REVOIR

HUGH FOX

ALL THINGS

THAT MATTER

PRESS

REVOIR

ISBN 13: 978-0-9840984-6-0

ISBN: 09840984-6-1

Library of Congress Number: 2009900658

Cover Design by All Things That Matter Press

Cover Photo by Leigh Blackall; Stencil by Anonymous

Published in 2009 by All Things That Matter Press

Table of Contents

"I don't see her! She said to get out of the baggage area on the north and that's where we are..."

"Such traffic! It's Las Vegas all over again. Thousands trying to get away from...I thought Phoenix would be more..."

Hundreds of cars, buses, taxis waiting, buzzing by, baggage on, baggage off. It was like Fest/Fiesta Las Vegas where she had just finished a three-day "course," call it "seminar", on pancreatic cancer, and he'd come along for the joyride, his seventy-fifth birthday today, February 12th...

"Only it doesn't seem like February...I thought it would be colder here..."

Laura Pathologist, impatient as always with Joey Poet, even worse now that he was retired and had larger and larger expanses of pure fun-time.

"What does she look like?"

"Well...she looked Spanish-ish...or maybe Greekish. Her parents were Flemish...country people, pas de Brussels...."

"As in Brussel Sprouts?"

"Exactly!"

"Very slanted, Thailandish eyes, black hair, a ski-slope nose, as thin as chicken legs."

"But she didn't cluck?"

"Stop making fun of her!"

"I'm making fun of you!"

"Brazilians can't ever be serious, can they? It could be doomsday and they'd still be samba-ing and slurping Tequila..."

"Not Tequila, please. Rum Whiskey! Or it could be Tequila..."

Suddenly a huge silver van pulls up in front of them and out steps an aged Madame-type, not really tubby, but just a little-little too chocolately-trufflish-pecan cheese cake-ish...but at the same time you could still see the traces of wild-forest exoticism, les forets, les sauvages de Flandres.

"You wouldn't happen to be Mr. Butterfinger-Coke, would you?" she Queen-Englished at him.

"So you saw The Queen, did you? I have an ex-student in California who looks exactly like her!"

And suddenly they were in each others' arms, "It's been eternities..."

"It's like the rebirth of the Roman Empire."

"The Resurrection and Ascension!"

Then stopping, Anne "taking in" Laura, "So you must be...if I may put it this way, THE ONE WHO GOT HIM!," giving Laura a hug too, standing back in "evaluating" her, "Not bad, plus exotique que moi...and a lot-lot-lot younger. The one that got him. I was married twice; the first one a furtive drinker who always picked his noise, the second one more ancient than the coliseum in Rome," laughing, perfect teeth, Joey wondering just how much cash went into them ivories...and gums, "not really, but dead five years now, in court on an almost daily basis until...."

A dark-blue-coated "guard/guardian" of some sort, wearing a dark blue almost police-ish cap, approaching them with exaggerated "official" alacrity.

"I'm sorry, ma'am, ma'ams, and sir, but you can't really tally here."

"'Tally?'" laughed Joey.

"Tally ho!"joined in Anne, literally jumping into the car with a grimace and a loud squeak of obvious pain, "So long, Stalin!"

"Sta...?" the guard obviously confused, "I didn't mean to..."

"You'll hear from my lawyer tomorrow," Anne straight-faced vicious, lead-weight serious.

"Ma'am...I...."

Anne said Joey and Laura, "Joey in the front seat, you, Laura, in the back-seat....it'll be 'safer' that way....more 'spread out'."

Laura almost rebelling, fighting back, but instead following orders, all the bags in the seat next to her in the back, and off they went as Anne stopped for a moment in front of the bewildered guard and threw him a kiss. Then off into traffic. And traffic there was, like La Guardia, O'Hare...even more so....

Out of Phoenix into the winter desert, Joey wanting to say "I've never seen a more depressing, dead desert, the California coast at times looks like this, but only at times......you ought to see the Japanese gardens Poet-temptress Ellaraine Lockie took me to in October. I was out in California writing this book about four genius California poets...," but didn't say anything, let her talk.

"It's 60's and 70's during the day here now, although we did have a biggy-biggy freeze last month, almost wiped out the oranges on my orange tree, but that's very rare. I go up to the mountains in the summer, have another place there. Mountains, trees, next to a lake. It's another world. It's a hundred and thirty here, never goes above seventy-five there. But it gets cold, cold, cold in the winter, and I've gotten to hate the cold. Two knee replacements, arthritis here and there..."

"I know. I just got castrated three years ago. Which would be okay if I still didn't have sexual impulses now and then...."

"Now and when?"

She laughs so boisterously that she almost swerves into the next lane, a guy in a top-heavy SUV honking at her. She gives him the finger, he honks back.

"Maybe you should just drive me back to a hotel" says Laura with Council of Nicea seriousness.

"What's wrong, my dear?" asks Anne with loads of caring in her voice.

Laura shrugging it all off, "It's nothing, just being a Brazilian here during the Great Depression Number Two. It's starting to make the '29 crash look like prosperity."

"So you know about gringo economic history?"

"She reads a lot," he explains, "she's all day looking through a microscope; in the evenings she likes to 'explore'..." Joey explains the soul of simpatía again, as suddenly Laura wasn't there at all for him and he had-had-had to ask, "Listen....why did we ever break up?"

"Do you think we...?" Anne all shyly circumspect, cautious.

"Talk about what you like, I can just close my eyes...and ears...I'm so tired anyhow. Not used to all this travelling. Usually it is just me and Senhora Microscope. No interaction with anyone."

And she closes her eyes. Instant sleep, the same as she always does in concerts, especially during Beethoven's late, post-deaf cello sonatos, and the minute the weather report comes on the evening, before-bed TV news, Joey looking back at her suddenly out-out-out, lowering his voice just a bit....

"Listen, Anne, how come we ever broke up anyhow? We were coming along strong, strong, strong, and then suddenly...."

"Well, I was going to Our Lady of the Rosary High School down by the University of Chicago. My father's idea...close to the university and all, you know. My old Flemish janitor father with an accent like a bandage around his mouth, and he wouldn't take anti-accent lessons from me....," laughing like crashing glass, then suddenly gets deadbeat serious again, almost teary-eyed, "Rosary High School, Sister Mary Rebecca...who they'd make fun of sometimes, Rebecca Old Testament, Rebecca, Rivka, and she was always tough-tough, there was this friend of mind, Terry McCarthy, came to class after lunch one afternoon, beer on her breath, even I could smell it, everyone laughing at her, I guess she'd gone home at lunchtime and her father was a construction worker, you know, sewers and the like, and Sister Mary Rebecca smelled the beer, slapped her, started screaming at her, 'Where did you get that beer?' Slapped her, pulled her hair...."

Stops, horrified like Frankenstein had just stopped in front of the car.

"Watch your driving!" Laura said from the back seat.

Anne calming down now, starting to sound like a psychiatric patient on a sofa again, talking to her resurrector psychiatrist, before the days of 'Take a pill, no need to talk about anything,' "So while I was in high school, no less, that had to happen, and you know Kirsch High, right? The 79th Street neighborhood, from sanctified to mundane schooling, mundane as in le monde...worldly....you see I did pick up a little Français from mes parents...but in public school...if any teacher hit you they'd end up in the brig," lauging, loving herself, her own language games, everything about herself, "the great school-ship of ordinariness...public, pubic...did I say that? Well, I started going up to Northwestern, I wanted to be a teacher myself. So I was going to college surreptitiously while I was in high school...and working as a waitress too...I hardly slept. No time for the likes of you..."

"The likes of me?"

Genuinely wounded. Too much like his mother or the nuns, always managing to wallop the zest out of him without even one finger-snapping blow. Which she picked up immediately. Part of the same system, n'est pas?

"Oh, I'm sorry I said that. I should have said 'No time for the likes of anything I liked...'"

"Ah, that's better!"

Back on the court again, ready for his next basket-try, looking at Laura in the back seat. Out again! The all-day-long effects of her sleeping pills and all the other pills she took, except the vitamins....58, going on 85.

"And then I met Howard in the student union one day. Coffee-break time. Studying business management. And he looked so busy-ness-like. I was convinced He saw my cat-eyes and he was hooked...."

"Of course you'd forgotten all about me, were out hunting, nest pas?"

"It's not me that was out hunting, my bio-chemistry was the huntress. We always act like, like we're so 'spiritual' everything, well-thought-out, logical, when all we are, are meows and ass....so we were married within a year and he had a job out here. I finished my degree and started teaching high school English, got pregnant with Mimi...La Boheme, my favorite, albeit tragic, opera...only it turned out that he was a..."

She stops, suddenly is on the witness stand and he's a wirey (rusted) old prosecuting attorney.

"He WHAT? What was his problem?"

"What wasn't his problem, black nyloned legs, a little sniff here, a little sniff there..."

"Sniffing women?"

"Whiskey, wine, gin, tequila...you name it, he guzzled it. And violent if contradicted. Forget sex, a lttle 'I love you'/ je t'aime,' once in a while. And sickish with the girls, always on the edge of..."

"Come on!"

"I just left before something happened, came out here, started teaching, got remarried, a widowered Luthern minister..."

"A Luthern minister? What happened to Catholicism? You were raised a Catholic..."

"He was a widower..."

"But Catholicism...."

"Here we are!"

A community with a high stone wall all around it, and you didn't just pull in but had to go through a gate, get okayed by a guard.

She waves. They know her like a sister. Three guards inside a stone cage. The gate opens.

"Impressive!"

Laura wakes up...stops faking her knock-out sleeping....

"What's happening?"

"We're here, Ms. Sleepy Eyes."

"I'm sorry; I had some beer on the plane. They didn't have malt beer, my favorite, but...."

"But Budweiser was wise enough. You ought to see her when she's back home on the job. Little blue pills every night, adding two years to her age every year."

He laughs. Anne Smacks him lightly on the cheek.

"Come on! She's your queen, after all!"

As Laura gets very interested in the "colony" they're driving in. All palms and coconut trees, orange trees, avocado trees, and the houses....

"What kind of houses are they?"

"Mobile homes, all of them, it's a mobile home community. Not fancy enough for you?"

"They're all fine. It's just that...,"Laura trying to be diplomatically Brazilian.

"That what?" Anne not grumpy as Joey would have expected her to be, her father being a Flemish-foreigner janitor in super-class-aware 30's and 40's Chicago.

"I don't know, looking at you, the way you talk talk, act...I almost said squeal...my English."

"The way I talk, squawk...you expected?"

"Corinthian columns, a Greek temple look...or an English Tudor, half-timbered look, or something Frank Lloyd ranchish...."

"You really know your architecture, don't you? I'm impressed..."

"We used to take classes at LCC...architecture...evening classes..."

"He's a frustrated architect," explains Laura.

"I thought you were a frustrated opera singer."

"Frustrated singer, dancer, saxophonist, skier, painter,

sculptor...basketball player...," he smiled.

"But he's not too frustrated as a you-know-what," Laura totally bright-eyed awake now. Whenever it was ridicule-time all her adrenalin went into high speed, "At least he wasn't until he got you know what."

"I don't know what, but I'd like to...fill in the blanks, there's only fifty-five years of them...."

"Fifty-five years of blanks, all of a sudden I feel posthumous...close to it."

"What are you talking about, your castration?"

As she pulls in front of her house, not too different from the rest, all of them about as alike as fifty papaya seeds inside a papaya.

"So this is it?"

"I'd like to know more about the castration."

A trailer in the driveway.

"So you go tailoring too?" he asks.

"More! More! More!"

She wouldn't let it go and once they'd gotten out of the car he solemnized it out like a death sentence.

"I had prostate cancer. They were giving me Lupron, I had a heart attack, a stint, started researching out Lupon and discovered a medical website that said it caused blood-clotting. So I went to my urologist and asked him what they did in the old days, before Lupron, and he said 'First of all, I didn't know about the Lupron problem, but the cancer is fueled by androgyne, so you get rid of the androgyne and you get rid of the cancer....' So I stretched out on the sofa in his office, opened my legs and said 'Snip away.'"

Anne beginning to laugh, out of control, the last thing he'd expected.

"It's not funny," he complained.

"It's really not!" Laura agreeing.

"So you're teaming up against me, the two of you!" Anne

opening the door, bowing for them to walk in. Which they did.

Perfect wood floors, a little computer "salon" off the left as you walked in, a huge sofa and plush-chaired (two of them) living room with a table between the chairs and the sofa, the living room leading into a carefully wood-cupboarded kitchen with an elegant high-tech electric flat-topped stove and metallic-surface fridge...another corridor that....

"Where does that lead?" asks Laura.

"Into the bedroom."

"And the door, over to the right?"

"The bathroom. A second door from the bedroom into the bathroom...."

Joey walking to a glass wall on the far side of the room, looking out at the lawn chairs and table in this two-walled, otherwise open space.

"A little atrium/summer room..."

"I'm never here in the summer..."

"Okay...autumn...call it spring-fall room!"

"Here it could be a winter room, practically. It never gets that cold, but...."

"When it's twenty-five and you think it's a warm day, you know you're in trouble," laughs Laura who can't stop eyeing every detail, turning around, ceiling to floor, as if she were trying to memorize it all for a test in architecture, "But it has nothing to do with a mobile home. Take a picture from inside and you'd never guess how it began!"

Anne reaches over and gives her a sisterly kiss. "Even though he's yours, I still dig you..."

"Dig me? As in grave?"

"Nothing grave, everything as ephemerally hilarious as it can get...So sit, sit, sit, you're home...chez vous...chez nous..."

"Chez vous is your home...and she changed it to chez nous...our home, that's a good sign," smiled Joey as he sat down, practically stretched out on the sofa. Just a bit tired himself too. Laura slumping down next to him.

"I'd love to have you both out here full-time," going over to the oven, opening it up, "toute parfait...perfect...I put it up to three fifty for forty minutes and then when it turned off it stayed warm, just a little more cooking, already on the plates, Japanese, they can take the heat. Careful now," carrying them over one by one with a big ugly mitt on her right hand.

Laura studying the table.

"Such a beautiful Corinthian wood-carved table with pilaster legs."

Showing off again.

"I usually eat at the kitchen counter...alone, alone, alone...my husband number two was such a doll. I could have moved out of here into a real Corinthian columned paradise somewhere, but....."

"Blessed are the humble, for they shall see God!" laughs Joey.

"Not Catholicism, but Joeyism!"

"What's all this?" Laura studying the contents of the plates now.

"It's salmon patties with a sprinkling of purple cabbage, a few long carrot strips, a sprinkling of broccoli, with still more sprinkling of Parmesan cheese, olive oil and, just for exoticism, a touch of Teriyaki sauce...and one last sprinkling of Greek herbs..."

"Very international!" Laura smiling, loving the Japanese dishes filled with beautiful geishas.

"Goulash! Like my grandmother!" smiles Joey.

"She wasn't Hungarian, was she?"

"Czech-Jewish, the same thing."

"And just a little gringo champagne," Anne struggling to open a bottle she'd taken out of the fridge after she's planted the dishes down in front of them.

"Here, let me have that!" Joey opening it with one quick

swish-pop, "Lots of practice..."

"Not much in recent years," Laura adds, "although he's still an irish Creme liquor guzzler."

Joey suddenly dead serious.

"I'll never get rid of the Irishman in me, she'll never get rid of the Brazilian-Azorian in her, you'll never really get rid of the Flemish in you...we carry our collective ancient selves unconsciously inside ourselves, even if we don't want to. Like my grandmother's Jewishness..."

"I feel like taking my plate outside and just eating my whatever-it-is goulash home-sweet-ommming in on the taste, escaping collective unconscious emeritus lectures on the collective, racial-genetic unconsciousness," Laura starting to get up.

"That's the end of it, end of lectures," Joey smiling, stuffing his face with the obviously heaven-sent food.

"I should be getting confused," smiles Anne, "but Ommmmming as in Buddhism and emeritus-- retirement with merit I just think you could have a lot of listeners...and Ommm-Sweet-Ommm...that's quite a circus-rider mastery of English."

"He's a great acrobatic English teacher!"

"Of everything but between-the-legness," Anne laughing, looking down between his legs, then suddenly getting very Japanesey slit-eyed like in the old seductive Chicago days, "although I bet before the cancer knocked him out, he was the heavyweight champion of the bed...."

"You didn't ever...?

"Not in the old days in Chicago which was like being in the year 1500, seventeen years before Luther and his...."

"Ninety-five theses nailed on the church door at Wittenberg, attacking the church for simony...selling salvation...."

"I'm impressed! How do you know such things?"

"Leo High School. We had a whole course on...the title of the book we used was The Protestant Revolution...Revolutionary or revolt, I forget which...," Joey getting crusaderish for a moment, then back to melting piety, "but I loved daily mass and communion, confession, the feeling you were saved, you died and went to eternal bliss with the trinity..."

"Mainly Jesus..."

"And all the saints," adds Laura, all tree of them getting up automatically-instinctively and hugging each other, "A little bit of it is smiling down on us right now."

"It's nice to have it back," smiles Joey.

The main-course disappearing 1,2,3,4,5, and then Anne went bustling into the huge freezer and pulled out these huge Japanesey-Geisha-ish bowls of....

"What's this?" Laura as always totally interested in putting tags on tastes.

"Praline ice-cream. I was going to mix in some cherry tarts or tart cherries, my goulashy way of seeing the world and all, but a voice inside me said 'PURITY IS BETTER THAN DIVERSITY.'"

Laura, was she kidding or just pulling on a serious mask?

"You're not talking about US, are you?"

"What do you mean?" Laura back in seventh grade again, surrounded by the nuns. "I'd love to live out here, escape the cold. Here and Brazil. Here in the winter and Brazil in the winter too, it's winter there when it's summer here," Laura's eyes all speculatingly wide, like she was looking up at a full moon.

"There is a new hospital opening here and they are looking for pathologists," Anne slurping up her ice cream, smiling.

"But what about...?" Anne smiling.

"Sex? Pardon me if I bring it up but he's androgeneless, I hate to say sexless...and post-post menopausal estrogeneless us...in a way it's the perfect time of life," Anne went on, getting very professorial, reverting to type...all we really are is mating mutton, matting wildcats, that's what we're all about, what everything alive is all about, from strawberries to giraffes, reproduction. We have our reproducing moment, moments, ten children was always my goal, although all I managed was two. We reproduce ourselves and when that's over, then it's time for walkers and NOT TO BE, waiting for death...but that's when our best humanness takes over, nothing between the legs, but plenty between the ears, in the mouth, skin against feather comforters in the dream, the way a certain street or house or hill or pond, stained glass window, chicken kabob looks/smells, the sense of being, another minute, hour, day, year, decade...however long we have. It's like full-time in the Louvre, the Nelson Gallery in Kansas City, the Art Institute in Chicago...everything is a museum, restaurant, a walk-along-the-lake gallery, or sometimes a film, best-definition possible TV, DVD's....and then we're gone....R.I.P., jahrzeits..."

"What do you know about jahrzeits?"

"Yiddish, jahr equals year, zeit equals time, year-time, memorial death-times, part of Kaddish...."

"What do you know about Kaddish?"

"Yitgadal ve yit kadash..."

She stops.

"You know the Hebrew prayer for the dead?"

"It's not really for the dead; it just praises God...for the dead is Catholic...Lutheran...."

"But how...?"

"My parents were Flemish Jews, got to the U.S., who asked questions? All the wars and...the German invasion of Poland in 1939..."

"Joey thinks my father was Jewish, one of my grandmothers admitted she was, we're Jews now, Joey's grandmother was a Jew who raised him as a fanatic Irish Catholic..."

"Amazing. So every time we dig another layer down, we find another link between us...the same foundation."

And they all embraced again, dessert finished.

"Any more coffee?" asks Anne.

"More everything," Joey looking lazier, more glutted, more tranquil, untwitchy than either of them had ever seen him before, "we need to talk about the new hospital that's looking for pathologists..."

"And the son who lives with you?"

"There's nothing wrong with the University of Phoenix. I've never watched a football or basketball or baseball game in my life, but I know the MSU team symbol....Sparty..."

"You can learn. You can learn...I have a little baklava, might you...?"

NOTHING LEFT TO FALL

"Do you believe at all in afterlives of any kind?" she asks as she starts to drink her poison.

Frail and cadaverish even before she starts, as if she doesn't really need to take anything to kill herself, as if all she'd have to do is close her eyes and wait.

"This is all the afterlife I want," he answers as he stretches out on the riverbank next to her, stretching out on the wild grass as if it were trimmed lawn, the river down at the bottom of the hill, winding through the forest like innumerable S's, no other houses close by, separated from everyone around them by at least a thick slice of forest. Not wanting total isolation, aloneness, but just a "pause," as he'd put it, between them and their neighbors.

They'd been looking for a house in France for years, every vacation, every time they'd had a chance to get away, Paris at first, but it was too touristy, "busy" with other Europeans and the ever-present gringo Americans, then the Parisian "suburbs" like Enghein, but the casino was there and nothing there really "grabbed" them, even the Lac des Cignes on the edge of the casino grounds just a bit too "commercial." And in Enghein there was no Notre Dame, Louvre, Seine, seaside either.

A couple of visits to Toulouse, but, again, like Marseilles, it was too "busy."

They wanted to escape, even before they'd found out they were both dying, just escape, get away, the Riviera was too Miami Beachish, they loved Provence, the Dordogne. One of her all time favorite pieces of music was Canteloube's Songs of the Auvergne, in the Auvergne dialect, long disappeared, but still traces of it in the accents of the Auvergnese:

soun, soun

like the Spanish

soño, soño,
sleep, sleep,

For a while she'd wanted to go back to Brazil, as she got older, find a job as pathologist there, and he could always, always, always teach English, but her brothers were all dead and one of her sisters had married a Chinese computer guy and was living in New York, which was the last place she wanted to go...to live, or to die...which was the way she had begun to think of all the places she was thinking of moving to...a place to live...and (not even or) die....

And France seemed to call them both. They'd started taking French at Lansing Community College, a Professor Clemente Goudiaby, a black from the Ivory Coast who had been raised in Paris, gone to the Sorbonne.

Other retirees in the classes, a Russian, a German, and one Lithuanian who never wanted to admit she was Lithuanian. Lots of young people. Even one of Lou's former students from Michigan State. Still loosely "bonded." Like Lou had told her, "It's something you never lose..."

They'd started watching French films every night. They both were retired, okay, but like Solange said "Writers never retire until the Angel of Death retires them," and he'd decided to do a book on French film.

"There's always a publisher out there in small-press-dom, looking for something that sings," she'd told him, and he had to agree.

Godard. Who they'd both hated. Truffaut. A little scarey. Chabrol. Too many "legs." But when they got to Renoir, especially Dejeuner Sur L'Herbe/ Lunch on the Grass, all set in Southern France, rivers and trees, full of the ancient, pagan, Roman and pre-Roman past, goatmen and prophecies, like something out of the ancient Andes or pre-Greek Greece, they fell in love with the whole idea of finding a magic place where they could escape to, out of analytical, electronic modern times, into a world where you somehow merge with the trees and the rivers and mountains and animals; you would emerge knowing what you were really all about.

Provence.

They'd "shopped around" for a long time, searching for the place to grow old in and die.

Loved the mountain at Les Baux-de-Provence, but it was too isolated, far from shops, restaurants, "fun."Saorge was magnifique, all mountains and "views," but "I don't know how long we'll be able to get around," he'd complained, "walking up and down the mountain streets all the time."

And she'd agreed, was already having troubles with her knees.

Even Arles, for all its almost Portuguese quaintness, was all rising and falling streets, a stroll a major workout.

They loved the Verdon river with its unexpected turquoiseness, but, as she said, "Thirty years earlier and we'd be all boats, and terraces overlooking the river, you know how much I've always wanted to live on a river, but now..."

The coast was "easier," but too touristy, busy, crowded. They wanted olive trees, lavender fields, vineyards, "people," but at the same time isolation, a face-to-face relation with, as he put it, "skies of couple-color, like brinded cows..."

Her correcting his quote, "'brindled,' not 'brinded.'"

His favorite poet (after Rimbaud)....Gerard Manley Hopkins.

And after going over Hopkins with her over and over again over the years, now that his memory was "faltering," she remembered him better than he did. Especially all the difficult, unusual words that he'd pointed out to her. Studying poetry the way he studied it was almost like looking through a microscope at a frozen section of a cancerous bowel.

So they'd found a place in Moustiers-Sainte-Marie, not far from the Grand Canyon du Verdon, on the edge of town, but close enough to still feel part of the town, meet people, "fit in" in a sense, even talked between themselves most of the time in French, with a dictionary always at hand.

"Que jour joli, j'aime beaucoup les fleurs ici, especialmente les roses/ What a beautiful day, I love the flowers here, especially the roses...," she'd said one day.

And he'd immediately corrected her.

"No 'especialmente' in French. Especially is surtout, " then added "Rien spécial avec les roses/ Nothing special with the roses, mais les...," reaching, with a touch of embarrassment, for his dictionary, a little hunting, and then "mais les toits de tuile rouges / The red tile roofs...," smiling, shifting into her native Brazilian Portuguese, "Vamos falar un pouco em Portuguese / Let's talk a little Portuguese."

He'd had one year teaching as a Fulbright Professor at the Sorbonne before he'd met her, and had met her when he was teaching for two years at the University of Santa Catarina in southern Brazil. But he'd never quite gotten rid of the Spanish accent he
picked up from his first wife of almost twenty years, a Peruvian from Lima. Every time he opened his mouth in Brazil he was immediately identified (wrongly) as an Argentinean. Although in France, they never quite figured him out; he could have been German or English, Irish, Czech. The Chicago he'd been raised in was "everywhere," and he'd had two Irish grandfathers, one German grandmother, another Czech-Jewish grandmother, had studied opera with a Viennese woman, piano with a Russian, German with a Czech...but French with a professor from the Sorbonne no less....

They'd settled in, made friends, felt as at home in Moustiere-Saint Marie as they'd ever felt anywhere, and then he started having problems urinating, she started having uterine pains.

"Just getting old," she said, and they'd lived with their growing pains for almost a year and then, when they'd gone to Cadiz in Spain in the middle of the winter to get away from a particularly irritating cold spell, they both found this huge, modern, impressive hospital, went and got checked, their insurance picking up 95% of the tabs, and they'd both been diagnosed with cancer, she for incurable uterine cancer that had spread into her liver and spleen and everywhere else, and he'd been diagnosed for esophageal cancer that had spread all the way down to his rectum.

The doctor had been very diplomatic.

"Podemos alleviar el dolor, prolongar el tiempo, pero 'curar' ...es un poco tarde para esto/ We can alleviate the pain, prolong the time, but 'to cure'...it's a little late for that..." Which she had immediately translated into French.

"Nous pouvon alleviar la douleur, prolonger le temps, mais guérir, il est une peu tarde pour aquelle...," more like she was in a French class working for an A, rather than having just received a death sentence.

Instead of despair they almost laughed at their resignation.

"It takes the indefiniteness out of it, doesn't it," smiled Lou.

"Yeah," she agreed, "Everyone dies, but it gets kind of confusingly fuzzy when..."

"The main thing is to get comfortable, let our deepest wants take over."

"Oh," she answered, more than the usual tears in her eyes, "I think we already have."

Which was very true for both of them. The house itself, the essence of Provence, just the right curves in the roof, the windows, the fountain in the garden, the old furniture they'd brought along with it, yellow and red walls, trees just where they should have been, the garden perfect for summer dusks that dragged on and on and on, lavender and roses and each other, a perfect bakery within almost comfortable walking distance, more and more friends to make, like the Parish priest, Father LeBlanc, Marcel Godard a local school master, all kinds of old women...and men...lots of kids, but mainly you got the impression it was almost a kind of 'old peoples' home...

"Americains...no pour visiter, mais rester...et il fait froid ici dans l'hiver,/ Americans...not visiting, but staying... and it gets cold here in the winter," said Clotilde, the woman who ran their favorite little bistro-bakery in town, the best coffees and cakes they'd ever, ever had.

"Froid, chaud..le plus important c'est vous...les gens, l'ambience., toute ensemble / Cold, hot...the most important thing is you, the people, the ambience, everything together," Lou had told her as he bit into one of her crumbly, delicious pieces of cake and slowly started sipping on the most concentrated and scrumptious coffee he'd ever tasted.

They'd never been happier. Not just the foods and the landscape but the sense that somehow they'd finally gotten inside it all, not just "culture" on the blackboard or computer screen or in books, but like it was a Jean Renoir film and they were part of it...full time. That was the best part of it, its full-time-ness.

Found a Dr. Thierry in town. Great with pain relievers. Very patient. As they got weaker and weaker he found an old widow who needed money, to help them out cooking, shopping, cleaning.

"How come she's our age and toute bien/ everything okay?" Solange complained one night as they were drifting off into sleep, spring moon, a nightingale, the window open, parfait / perfect.

"It's like my grandmother...she was ninety-one and still going strong. It's genetic. And work. Maybe the worst thing we could have ever done was to retire. Or retire from teaching and medicine and start delivering mail." Which got her giggling.

REVOIR

The nightingale stopped and all that was left were the sounds of crickets and the sounds of leaves in the minimalist breeze. They always slept in each others' arms. Nothing sexual. Like children. One light kiss and then off they went.

BETHLEHEMANIA

"The problem is," said Pope Jesu I (2022) to the College of Cardinals, very good Italian, although he was Czech, having studied in Rome when he was a kid where is father was working for Chinoise International ("We make even the undreamt of!"), "the problem is that everyone identifies Catholicism with Rome. So we got rid of Latin, we've got to go back to Jesus' language, have our headquarters where Jesus was born."

"But that's Israel now!" says Bishop Joseph Pollard from L.A., originally an Irishman, but you'd never guess it hearing him talk after fifty years of "Los Angelesification," as he always put it.

"So we can buy Bethlehem, we've got the money."

"But it's so small," objected Cardinal O'Sullivan from NYC, "I mean the Vatican, you know, the whole thing..."

Suddenly the Pope, getting as solemn as the Great Wall of China, the Roman Coliseum, The Way of the Cross, Jesus walking on water....

"For millennia, the Catholic Church has been the Roman Catholic Church because it began at the end of the Roman empire. But what it really is the Ecumenical Catholic Church which, if you fine-tune it, means the Jesus-centric Catholic Church, born where Jesus was born, in Bethlehem. The Jews have Mount Sinai and Moses, we have the Israel-Bethlehem Jesus-is-born-centrism...after all the scandals recently we have to redefine ourselves, relocate, the Vatican can stand, St. Peters can stand, but I want to re-zionize the whole thing...we got rid of the Latin Mass, why not the Mass in Hebrew, bring the Jews into the church with us, show them that the Messiah has already come, no need to wait around for him. After all, the first Christians were Jews who switched and become Christ-ians, let the rest of them switch too, end all anti-semitism...as (and here his voice slowed down and almost turned into a frightened whisper) let us assume the place of the persecuted along with the converted Jews, let's see if anti-Semitism is based on Christ-rejection or not...Christ wasn't a Roman, the Romans killed him, why should the center of Christness be in Rome?"

Some agitation among the cardinals, but there was a certain logic in the whole thing, wasn't there, and most of the cardinals were sick of the Mass in local languages, Latin gone the way of all flesh, no more organs, instead pianos and guitars, women passing out the hosts, the body and blood of Christ, and everyone just chewing them like a roast beef sandwich, they wanted back, back to before reform-modernization, back, back as far as you could go...which was the Jewish-Jesus, nicht wahr?

> Baruch atta Adonai
> Elohainu Melech
> Haolam, Borei Pri
> Hagafan.....

> Holy Art Thou, Oh Lord,
> Creator of the Fruit of
> the Vine....

The blesséd wine...the communion services already in the Old Hebrew Services, the blessing of the wine, Christ's blood.....

There was some minority displeasure in the College, especially among the Romans...even Sicilianos...and the super-traditional Portuguese, but there were no Martin Luthers in the crowd, everything "passed," as it were, and the negotiations with the Israelis began.

Prime Minister Moses Horowitz: "Israel for the Israelis. Look at Gaza, no more incursions, 'outsiders.'"

Pope Jesu I: "No Catholic violence against Israel so far, just the Moslems, but it could begin, regalvanize the Catholic Church, forget about all the priestly infractions against the Natural Law, revive the Crusades..and, besides, do you have any idea of how much money could be involved, and tourism....look at what all that DaVinci nonsense brought in, and would the Arabs still attack worldwide Christianity...think of all the peaceful Arabs in Detroit, New York, Boston....have you ever been to the magnifique Arabs markets in Paris?"

Horowitz: "How much 'territory' are you talking about?"

Jesu I: "One square block. We don't have to build 'out,' we can build 'up'...toward the Trinity, in Nomine Patria, Filius et Espiritu Sanctus..."

Horowitz: "Which I hear you're going to turn into Hebrew?"

Jesu I: "The language of Jesus!"

Horowitz: "Aramaic, that was the language of the time of Jesus. Kind of a modernized Hebrew. We still use it in the Kaddish, the...

Jesu I (Interrupting him): I know, the prayer for the dead.

Horowitz: Not exactly for. A remembrance. We believe in an afterlife, but don't know much about it....

Jesu I: You ought to convert to Catholicism, then you'd know...

Horowitz: "You're not going to try to..."

Jesu I: "Convert Judaism into Christianity? We're just two beefs from the same herd, one (you) with udders, the other (us) with horns.

Horowitz: "I don't like the sound of that, too much goring right now."

Jesu I : "It's just a metaphor."

Horowitz: "What we'll want are exact figures viz a viz space, how much you'll be able/willing to pay, your intentions, limitations, restrictions, the whole, total picture...Okay?"

Within a month Jesu, or Jesus, as many of his colleagues called him, some of them even saying that he was the real Jesus, this was the Second Coming, we were close to the end of the world....within a month, Jesu-Jesus had come up with all the things Horowitz had asked for. And then some! And the picture emerged of Israel ending up at the top of the tourist trade/pilgrimage trade, Catholics, Christians of all breeds coming in to visit Christ's birthplace and all the rest, their minds "back in place, time to forget Luther's break with Rome, Henry the Eighth's wives and the formation of the Church of England, Methodism, the Baptists, the Albigensians/Cathars/KnightsTemplar...whatever...history beginning again where it should have begun in the first place...."

Even a little applause, Cardinal Greskovitch (Budapest) talking to Cardinal Repasky (Poland), "I like his vision...in the beginning...in principio...it's time to begin again."

The buildings were built approaching sky scraperish, Frank Lloyd Wrightish twenty story concrete block monsters with Constantinopolitan spires on top. The Catholics were on the world news every night, there was talk about the Boston parishes (some of them) going to re-open, there was talk of Quigley Seminary reopening in Chicago, everything slowly going back into sanity, The Divine Order.

"Not bad here in Israel," Jesu Primero,thinking after he'd gotten his new bedroom all settled, huge bed, huge candles on each side of the bed, but a snap-off switch for the overhead and reading lights on a hand-carved mahogany beside table. A little of Nyquil, a final reading of the middle of the second chapter of The Apocalypse, half a page of Talmud, Baruch Atta Adonai...sleep well, doors all double-locked, alarms on....and off he sank into all-is-right-with-the-worldness....

Then about five the first bomb blast, or was it a rocket...

If it had been up to him he would have just re-closed his eyes and drifted off into more sand dunes of deepest sleep, the Realist in him not the slightest surprised or perturbed...not after Henry the Eighth had tied Blessed Oliver Plunkett's arms and legs to four horses and pulled him apart after cutting open his belly and pulling out all his guts, real happenings in real (historical) time...only there went the alarms, banging on the door.

In the beginning was the Word and the Word was God and the Word was with God and the Word was....

BANG!

Pulling on his robe and painfully moving toward the door....

MONKEYSHINE

"Come in, come in, come in," said Alexander's step-grandmother, Azariah, midget-monkeyish, pequeñissimo, "It's so good to have you here for the Fourth of July. All the way from Boston!"

"Cambridge, si vous plait," Alexander corrected his step-grandmother, "Cambridge isn't Boston, just like earth worms aren't Sir Galahad," black shoes, knee-high black socks, black shorts, blue, long-sleeved shirt, with a tie no less, his mother Charlotte always preaching, "The child's image is the adult's reality, you want him to be General Patton, you dress him in khaki, you want him to be a cockatoo you dress him in feathers.."

"Only you're looking and sounding too serious, pal. You lookook like a maudit lawyer-doctor," groaned grandpa Ryan, Mr. Irisher-Chicago, "kids oughta be kids, there's time enough to be old, bald, bold, bowled-over."

"You look like you're been bowled over," answered Alexander, five, just three days after his fifth birthday, running over to grandpa and punching him in the stomach as in come Mama Charlotte and Alexander's older sister Pocahontas (8).

"Really, dad, you always dressed me like Madame Serieux when I was a kid. Remember Spain and the Azores and Lisbon, Campeche, everyone would call me Señora and Madame...half-jOking but half serious..."

"And look at you now, married to a Parisian, teaching German philosophy at the University of Harvard," Ryan loving the complexity of his daughters' and sons' lives, his own life, complexity, complexity, complexity, like a giant electronic interstellar chess-game, staring as serious as he can at Alexander, "So do you play the bagpipes, my friend? And where's your kilts and Scotch beret."

"My mother got her Ph.D. from Edinburgh....but before I was even born. And besides the past is the past, Scotland isn't all just folkloric I.D. anymore...."

Pochahantas coming in with FORCE now, usually playing distant, wistful, hard-to-get, but when ignored....

"I play the drums and I don't need a kilt. I've got my Scotch plaid skirt, and...."

She started skipping, jumping, hopping around, whistling the whole time.

"Nicely done!" applauds grandpa, then suddenly seriouses out with Charlotte, "But where's Claude?," walking out into the hallway sniffing around, "Didn't he come with you?"

"N....n...n....." struggle-stumbles out Charlotte, "he's at a French conference in the French Antilles. You know how it is, conferences equal publications equal, raises equal tenure, equal sanity...although...."

"He hates me because of my hairlip...et je ne peut pas parle le française sans un accent Portuguese!"

"I can translate that!" Pocahantas solemn now, Bill Gates-ish ladling out his billions to Jesus Christishly save the world, "because I can't speak French without a Portuguese accent."

"How can you be so serious so young?" asks grandpa, taken aback, like he was watching pool balls on a pool table playing pool ball by themselves.

"I can be serious too," Alexander blurts in, looking up at the ceiling. "It's a bird, it's a plane, it's Saddam Hussein...."

Grandpa falling down on his knees, "Baruch atta Adonai, in nomine Patria, Filius et Espiritus Sanctus, Amen...may the words of my heart never, ever fart...all I want is NOW, NOW, NOW...for forever somehow...."

"Sea turtles live three hundred years," Alexander began to lecture, "Why should there be such a difference between aquatic animals and terrestrial mammals? Why should mammiferous mean whisperous, if I may coin a word?" taking a deep breath, ready for round two.

"Time for bed, my friend, " Azariah cuddling him around the ears.

"My God, these kids are internet encyclopedias," says grandpa, utterly flabbergasted, "When I was a kid it was roast potatoes in the empty lot next to our apartment house, and biking through the rain, a little whizzing through OZ, but...how will it be in another three thousand years?'

Pequeñina Azariah suddenly beginning to cry, solidified, petrified, mummified, except for crying, and then Mama Charlotte doing the same.

"What's going on?" Grandpa all mystified, confused.

"Another three thousand years," wept La Professora, "with the way things are going now? Nuclear proliferation, the old all gone, planetary warming, changes in the earth's weight, will it go closer to the sun...into the sun? Or fly further into outer space? Burnt up or frozen up? Or self-destroyed, or..."

"Come on! Come on!" Grandpa embracing everyone, "three thousand, thirty thousand, a million thousand thousand...Baruch atta Nothing At All!"

And maybe it was his tone, his all-encompassing caring, the all-encompassing everything-do-wellness in his words, but slowly they all calmed down and grandpa went into the fridge and got out some Moose Track ice cream, dark-chocolate and vanilla, and they all found places in the living room, sat down and he turned on the weather channel (Hysteria Season) and they began to yum-yum through the very aristocratically special ice cream.

Then Alexander very "officially" gets up and turns the TV off, sits back down and begins to officiate again.

"I have some insomnia problems. You should know, it's genetic. Too bad it can't be engineered out of the gene-bank. And

I'm getting immunized to my usual sedatives, and besides, I'm leery of negative side-effects, and...."

"Stop!" says grandpa, goes into the refrigerator and finds a butter-pecan ice cream bar that's been dipped in chocolate, Alexander's favorite combination.

"Pour toi, mon ami!/ For you, my friend," and he hands the bar to little serious boy face, almost evOking a smile from him.

"That's more like it, Grandpa, to the diablo with cholesterol and 2% milk. Remember how you told me your Czech grandmother lived on lard and lived to be a hundred and thirteen...."

"Well...she had trouble with numbers...but you don't forget anything, do you," grandpa sitting down on the sofa next to Alexander.

"I'm Mr. Megabytes when it comes to memory."

"But I don't understand, you don't have a TV because your father said that if he had one he'd do nothing else but watch hockey all day, and he's supposed to be writing books on French literature....so you speak French at home, n'est pas?"

"Oui,nous toujours parlons le français chez nous./ Yes, we always speak French at home."

"And you're in pre-school, right?"

"Right as Martin Luther rebelling against simony," he answers with a smirky sneer.

"Wait a minute, I mean WAIT-A-MIN-UTE, nobody, but nobody knows about Martin Luther and simony...."

"Except Lutherans and me!"

"But you're Jewish!"

Charlotte came down the stairs after having quietly vanished for a few minutes, all dressed in a flowered dress and flowery sandals, a Ph.D. in German philosophy, sure, but before she got serious she'd spent five years in Hollywood trying to get into films, forty-five now, but still a looker, although she had had a few eye- and lip-tucks when eyes and lips began to drag and down curve just a little.

"I don't know if I like the tone of that!"

"But I'm Jewish, too..."

"But these days...."

"OKAY...," Grandpa turning his tone into pure Michigan maple syrup poured on Mexican cinnamon-dosed papaya," but you're Jewishish, too..."

She goes into the kitchen, takes a little black, sugarless coffee from the coffee machine that she keeps going from dawn to midnight, sits down on a sofa at a right-angle to grandpa and Alexander.

"Listen, the way that monkey talks. I mean his vocabulary, even the 'delivery' style, he's more like an octogenarian than a five year old...," whines grandpa, marveling at how his super-brain daughter still remains an all-star beauty, with all her dimples and vampire-black eyes, a body like a combination of cow and a salamander.

"Nonogenarian! More like a nonogenarion...or centenarion... of course with a little old man amnesia," Alexander spits out with wild vehemence, like an old Buick 9 honking at midnight on New Year's Eve.

"See! Where does he pick it up?"

"Well, he goes to a public pre-school in Somerville. You know, Ethiopians and Sudanese, Gringo blacks, Moroccans, Armenians, Greeks, Portuguese, Brazilians, Cubans, Peruvians... two or three Irishers..."

"That's the way Chicago was in the old days. English was the foreign language."

"It's better that way."

"Mais, je prefere le français/ I love French," she sighs out romantically, memories of France obviously skittering through her mind.

"No need to translate for grandpa, he understands French," Alexander unexpectedly defending grandpa with a great deal of tough-guy vehemence.

"Pero tu no entiendes Español.../But you don't understand Spanish..."

"No tienes que traducir nada para me, entiendo todo. / No need to translate for me, I understand everything."

"But where did he, how did he.....pick up all those languages?" screams Grandma Azariah.

"Well, he knows some Sudanese too, some Ethiopian, which is getting kind of arabicized...remember King Solomon in Ethiopia...," his mom explains condescendingly, Ms. Multi-Linguist herself.

"But...," grandpa ruminates philosophically, psycho-therapeutically, "It's not just vocabulary but delivery. He sounds more serious than an ecumenical council...."

"Winston Churchill!" adds Azariah.

"Oh, we can be silly-willies too," chuckles Alexander and grabs his sister's arms, "a little terpsicore-time, Alicia...," and they both begin to dance.

"Alicia?" Grandpa all confused.

"Markova! Check her out on the internet search."

"Net-search?"

Both of them ignoring grandpa's confusion, starting a little Fred Astairish-Ginger Rogerish singing-dancing:

> We may be weird,
> but we're not alone,
> who's that weirdo
> on the telephone?

We know too much
in a dumbass world,
so keep it rippled
and keep it whirled.

One for the money,
two for the show,
and listen to
that grandpa wind
blow.

He thinks he's a genius,
and almost is right,
but one thing he can't do
is stand up and
fight...

As they go on Grandpa whispering to Charlotte, "But are they 'improvising?'"

"No, they write plays in school, take dance and performance classes. It's all very audience-oriented."

"Very impressive," and grandpa sits back, closes his eyes.

"Is he sleeping or just listening? Is he alright?" Charlotte asks Azariah.

"We've all gotta go sometime, that's just realism," she answers, sits down next to him and closes her eyes too, as the two kiddies continue to dance and sing:

Wir müssen sterben
jetz oder später,
Ich wollte ein engel

sein, wo später ist
niemals....

We must die
now or later,
I'd....

Trying to sing the translation too as Grandpa opens his eyes and almost sits straight up.

"You do great in English, rhyming and all...," then eyes close again and he collapses into total relaxation.

"I agree," says Azariah, not moving at all.

The kids keeping singing.

They might be dead,
but aren't we all,
that's the story of life,
one, two, fall.

Do it while you can
all you've got to give,
one thing you haven't,
an eternal life to
live...

Grandpa still wondering how they could manage to sing so perfectly together, still not believing it came out of the school, but that they were improvisatory geniuses. Between them they sounded by a combination of Steven Foster and some kind of Celtic connection. Or had Charlotte sadistically/prophetically written the whole show?

DON'T LOOK UP/WAKE UP! the voices inside him said, time for a little break, turn off the computer-calculator brain....snooze, booze, nothing to lose...Began to snore, wasn't really sure if it was genuine or just more theatrics. It was in the genes, n'est pas?

TOO NICE

The trouble with Maggie is she's too nice. Want some fancy words? Okay. Altruistic, psychologically permeable, self-effacing, Freudian. Okay, lemme give you an example. Al, her youngest, sees a cat out in the back yard. Stranger cat. It's fur in all kinds of funny little black and white scribblings. You've seen horses like that, haven't you?

Okay. He goes out.

"Lemme water the clematis, no rain for three weeks."

He's only five but he sounds like some kind of 1920's Wall Street giant, always watching the DOW and all that stuff. It's his father, Mr. Big Investment Frenchman. But at the same time, it's like the kid himself is bewitched. His father's too serious and his jack-in-the-box treacherousness is a reaction to the boredom that usually reigns in the house. No TV, a mini-computer you can play DVD's on, but they all have to be French films, and the kid's only six. You see what I mean?

Out into the backyard he goes with this old mesh bag he got out of the garbage that was filled with potatoes. A sardine in one hand that Maggie doesn't see or notice. The bag? Well, a bag's a bag, kids are kids and play with bags, she doesn't want to get all weighed down with finickyness.

He holds the sardine in one hand, the bag in the other, and when the cat comes to get the sardine, he plops the bag down over it, let's it get the sardine first, that's in his favor, right? But then, once it's in the bag, he pulls it up by the top, the cat tries to claw him, a little success, a little blood, but he runs over to the pond in the back yard and throws the cat in.

Maggie hears the cat screaming, the splashing, finally comes out, the cat is scrambling around, drowning in the pond.

"What in Baruch Atta Adonai's name are you doing, have

you done?"

"Just a little hunting practice."

Which she ignores, tries to lift the bag up and let the cat crawl-jump out, but no go. A couple of scratches on her hand, sprints into the house and comes back with a huge beef-brisket - cutting-scissors and carefully cuts one strand of the bag, then another, the cat always trying to (unsuccessfully) claw her, until the bag is just a pile of strings, and the cat silently slips into the bushes and is gone.

"I suppose you're gonna string me up from a tree. Execution by hanging."

"Where do you learn all that crap?" At first angry, ready to, for the first time ever, slap him, and then suddenly filled with a sense of awe.

"You're such a weird kid. I don't know where you get your language, tone, whole manner of 'delivery.' It's the maturity, beyond good and evil, just your 'adultness.'"

"It's not adultness," he laughs, "all monkey-rats have the same 'delivery.' Films, class, TV...and Papá. Je suis exactemente comme mon papá..."

Which hits Maggie between the eyes, thinking, yes, it was true, he was just like Claude, Claude a little less veiled and hypocritically double-dealing but under all of Claude's mannerisms and masks, what was he beside Mr. Baby Brat?

"Okay, my friend, let's go for some ice cream."

You see what I mean? You encourage the little monster to be a little monster and what happens when he grows up. I mean.....

"What do you mean you're innocent? Your fingerprints were on the gun. She scratched your cheek in a gesture of last minute desperation, and the blood under her fingernails matched yours one hundred percent. We have witnesses who saw you come out of the house, witnesses who were sitting on lawn-chairs in the front yard next door to your victim's house. I don't see why we even need a jury. This is as obvious as a vintage Lincoln penny, a sunrise over the Sierra Madre..."

"I tell you, I'm...," suddenly he breaks down and starts to cry, "OKAY...OKAY....she said. "She was going to leave him and I'd invested my entire emotional life in the dream of us being together. And then when it came time to leave him, she backed down.

"It's mainly money," she said, "We can get together when he's not around but...."

"No buts about a bullet in the brain, n'est pas?

The judge gets up, walks over to the jury.

"I'm not really supposed to do this. Distance, impartiality, let the lawyers do the boxing. But I've never seen a more boxed-up-to-prison case in my life. Like when I was a child and...Okay this potato bag and...let it go at that. Ça sufit...sufit....don't forget the Norman Invasion of England. Three-quarters of English is cognate with French...time to deliberate, talk things over..."

IN THE NAME

"In the name of the Mother, the Daughter and Grandmother Moon," Hermione barely able to talk, much less make the Sign of the Moon over the Winter Equinox Feast, a whole roast lamb with roasted potatoes all around its ribs and shanks, a moon-glow candle stuck carefully in its belly.

Something Sigmund had objected to.

"What if it spills and the wax...."

"You want Spring back, don't you?" she answered, barely, lisping, murmuring, but as adamant as the Escorial, the Alhambra, Machu Picchu. So he just lets it go.

Wife number two, the Professor of Comparative Religion who hadn't taught for thirty years, Forgetfulness Disease and knee and back horrors, fears, "Who am I? Where am I going? They're all against me!"

Like a big fat rotting peach on legs, but Miranda (Wife # 1) and Delicia (Wife #3) loved her, and Hermione was great with her grandkids, Margarete, Menina, Leo, Thor, and Grandiose, as well as her kids, Wanda, mother of Margareta and Menina, Philco, father of Leo and just-married Cannonball, father of Thor and Grandiose...as well as all kids of the other wives...not to mention the second husbands....the lists kept going on and on and were always growing......

All lived in St. John, Michigan and facing them all together for the Spring Equinox Fiesta that coincided with the Mint Julep City Fest; sometimes she felt like she was a football player looking up at the stadium crowds, a Sioux chief on a mountain looking down at invading Yankee cavalry, a ballerina on stage, one last Petrushka twirl and the audience would go crazy.

Long John, the once-super-macho husband of them all, sitting down at the long primitive wood-slab table and carving off a piece of lamb leg, smiling victoriously, all eighty-five years of barely-held-together said, "Magnifique lamb! We never should have broken up. All Delicia knows how to cook is birds, birds and Tainha!"

"What"s Tie-eenya?" asked Gordua, verging on 500, totally paranoid like her mother, Miranda.

"Brazilian fish! Tainha!," screamed Miranda, sucking on an ice cream bar she found in Hermione's fridge. Miranda loved Hermione's fridge, everything about Hermione's Alden Dow house with all its space, space, space, everything paid for by Delicia, who owned an eternal Luso-Brazilian-Japanese fish trading company she'd inherited from her Brazilian father.

Sigmund got very solemn. Not really solemn, nothing really "real" about him but his sperm.

"Eat, my multiplied darlings! Don't dilute the glory of the lamb with small talk. And besides, the festival awaits us! As it does every year...," his voice suddenly became mouse-salamander small, a whispering cloud instead of a howitzer, "not that I want to talk about years....here in the glory of wives and sprouting offspring, a whole new world to colonize the future...and moi?"

Hermione, Miranda and Delicia all coming over to him and comforting him as his obsessive death-thoughts began to descend upon him, like he'd every night spend his dream-time with his long lost friends like: Jean Anne Kappel (black hair, black eyes, Mr. Orient smile, him 10, her eight) and Joe Petruccio (Mr. 400 pounds, "have another pizza!," not a piece, but the whole, him 15, Joe 16); Richard Morris, him 60, Richard 58, Mr. Nuclear Physicist-Astronomer-Dreamer in San Francisco, "Will the couch be okay for you?;" Noel Peattie, him 70, Noel 85, Noel asking him one day in Santa Monica, "Do you really think I'm the greatest poet-thinker in the twentieth century...?," names, presences, him always travelling, here, there everywhere, but nowhere like coming back to home-sweet-St. John's Mint Julep home.....all the wives in unison "You'll be fine, you'll be a hundred, there are people who live to be a hundred and twenty five...."

Delicia's daughter Papaya's son, Stone (as in Stone Peak, Mr. Top of the Mountain) coming up and giving him a hug, "You're the greatest grandpa ever-never, any-stormy weather."

Which turned him back into butterflies and black-eyed susans again, stood up and gladiatorially shouted, "Okay, everyone dig in! I wanna see some bones, no more flesh." Huge deluges of laughter and everyone literally attacked the lamb and potatoes.

"Ein, zwei, drei....zehn,
It'll never be a lamb again."

Sitting down happily, everyone eating like the Third Reich was going to dump them in ovens if they slowed down, then time for MINT ice cream, muffins, doughnuts, tea, pop....and when everyone was puffed up with foodies, beginning to sit back and blithefully relax into gluttony-splendor he stood up and almost militarily (again) announced.

"Okay, meine freunden, my dear extensions of our blood, time for the Mint Julep Festival. It's only a few blocks away in the auditorium of the high school, and I bought advance tickets because we'll half fill the place up...and this holy, genetic multiplication....it's what it's ALL about..."

Tears in his eyes, and they all began to applaud, whistle, Stone busy again, "You're a grandpa that ain't no downpour, just a drifting mist of pure Mint Julep joy!"

More, louder applauds and "Wooos," and "You bets" and "Right ons."

Out the front door of his Michigan natural boulder Bavarian-looking castle-house, helped along by his three wives who got a little help themselves from their kids and grandkids, still a little light, the sidewalks peppered with others going to the festival, just looking at all the old German-Dutch-English-Irish faces, some of them in their nineties, all bundled up against the still-cold, but benignly smiling, lots, lots, lots of them hello-ing and howyadoin'-ing him, faces he'd known for what seemed centuries, feeling a kind of Christmasy-Easterly PEACE descend upon him, the old round faces and perfect white hair, little round hats, glasses, coats just short enough.long enough to show legs and boots, the legs always perfect, although under the pantyhose you never knew....

The three wives muttering-murmuring together, It's so beautiful, look at the moon coming up, full-moon, twilight moving into night, then handing the ticket-taker at the door all the tickets.

"I've never seen anything like this!"

Another Deutsch-Dutch round face.

"Just a little family."

"Schön, schön,schön/ beautiful, beautiful, beautiful...."

Going into the magnifique recital/show time auditorium, magnifique like everything else in St. Johns, even thinking "saintly," so many old grandmas and grandpas, kids, grandkids, more "Hi's," what was it, pan-Germanic prejudice, racial bigotry, he wondered, but the voices came back singing to him like the Rhine Maidens in the ring operas, "What it is, is the peace...it all goes by like the twinkling of an eye, a hundred years like a day, there's no time for anything else but...," sitting down, for a moment closing his eyes ("Is he alright?," "He's not losing consciousness, is he?") and seeing the world outside the town, the endless roads going through fields of just-ready-to-be-harvested mint, corn, soy, you-name-it, the hundred-plus-year-old farmhouses and bars, the deer in the forests between the farms, deer and wild turkeys, swamps, cattails, rivers, esker-hills that take your breath away, it was like living in ancient heavens slumbering in eternal peace, sanity...

A woman came in the auditorium with a little girl, her white

(Greek?), the girl mulataish....and tears came into his eyes...more sanity...one, mixed-everyone country instead of a hundred countries, a hundred primitive tribal-war worlds...

BRONZE

After lunch, nap, alt, alt, alt,/old, old, old, Deutsche still coming in once in a while, a little schnapps and Michigan turned into Bavaria...or the Andes. Stretched out on his bed, a distant train out there, a little rain, but....the more he stretched out the more he thought about Tiawanku, the Bolivian highlands, ANAKU, the land across the ocean from the ancient misnamed "Old World," where the apples of immortality grew, remembering the mountains and the forests, los indios speaking Quechua, almost the same as Arabic, APU Inca, Father Inca, and the Arabic ABU for father....just drifting off into cloudland, when there was a knock on the front door.

The postman? Insufficient postage on one of his return envelopes? Slowly struggled to his feet and walked to the front door and looked through the front-door window.

Miranda!

Thought she was still in Peru. Seventy-eight, going on two-hundred, trying to remember that face fifty years back when he first met her in Cuzco when he'd gone there on vacation, Machu Picchu, the whole Andes, sitting at a cafe drinking coca tea and knitting a poncho, "Can I join you?"

And she answered, "Why not?"

"How come you know English, everyone study English."

"Studies! That's what I just said."

"No, you didn't." And that's how it had all begun....not began....

Opens the front door.

"What a surprise!"

"Just back from Cuzco, thinking about you...."

"I've been thinking about you too. Every night owl-you comes in through the window and starts to hoot..."

She laughs.

"I'd do more than hoot, even at seventy-four..."

Into the parlor, the big sofa in front of the huge TV, but she didn't want that, moved into the dining room and sat down at the table, pulling the chair out, facing him.

"How about a little...," pauses, lets him fill in the blanks.

"A little Irish Creme?"

"Not too little..."

He goes and gets two antique Czech glasses, Czech crystal from his grandmother, pours out ample glassfuls, which she savors carefully, then half-whispers,

"We should get remarried. Forgive me for my sins."

"And you forgive mine."

They melt into each others' arms, his adultery and second marriage to the adulterous partner, her lying to him about an earlier marriage and three children she never mentioned to him before they got married, all forgotten now, they were freshly washed silverware, freshly washed plates and cups, an Andean feast of all the right Datura-Coca herbs that made hundreds year olds common in the Peruvian-Bolivian-Ecuatorian mountains.

"Tanto tiempo que he esperado este momento/ Such a long time that I've waited for this moment."

She laughs.

"We're still not really ONE!"

Which he doesn't take laughingly but with severe seriousness.

"Que quieres decir con esto?/ What do you mean to say with that?"

"You sound more Argentinean than Peruvian. And not from Buenos Aires or La Plata either, but from cow-country, sun-flower country."

Still laughing, "The best beef in the world, not one ounce of 'cultivated' food, everything sylvestre/ wild...."

"Like the both of us!"

She grabs and hugs him, both of them surprised by her strength.

"One body, one spirit....tribal unity the way it should be, all the tribes in the world in their little circles, surrounded by a little empty space....and let's concentrate on other things besides annihilation..."

"As in 'nihil,' he smiles back, 'nothing,' nothing at all...," as they move into the kitchen and he opens the freezer door, filled, filled, filled with shrimps and salmon, tapas, lentils, mujadara, zatar pie...and a hundred different flavors of ice cream.

RIVE GAUCHE

Becoming Fallish, the Rive Gauche, cafes, cafes, cafes, always the river, almost all the leaves gone, me and my favorite place, Le Chat Minuit/The Midnight Cat, angry-eyed Baudelaire with his usual stubble, bald, with his back-hair combed as usual up to the front, if not to "hide" the baldness, at least to confuse the eye a little, waiting for me.

"How's it going?" An embrace.

"Travelling, like always."

"Traveling?" pointing to his head, "I don't even care where as long as it's new, Heaven or Hell, what's the difference? Into the Unknown to find the New, / Enfer ou Ciel, qu'importe? Au fond de l'inconnu pour trouver du nouveau."

Verlaine, as usual bearded, bald, "robust," his penetrating eyes looking right through me to the universe beyond, walking by just as I'm ordering a glass of cabernet sauvignon and a crepe, more embraces, kisses on the cheeks.

"Foxy, howya doing?"

"Okay, good to see you..."

"Don't worry, the moon is red...water flowers fold their petals, pale, Venus appears and it's night./La lune est rouge au brumeaux horizon, les fleurs des eaux referment leurs corolles, blanch, Vénus émerge, e c'est la Nuit."

"That's more like it, man, take it the way it is, no elaborations," I answer, he smiles.

"I do what I can."

To which Baudelaire answers, "I do what I can't."

"I hate to say it," says Verlaine, "but what can't you really do?"

Everyone laughs as Valery, Corbiere, Mallarmé, Poulenc, Nadie de Boulanger drift by, just a little bit too light, fragile.

I try to wake up, grit my teeth, slap my cheeks, but no gritting, no pain, and I slowly begin to realize I'm not "sleeping" at all.

Feeling Friday afternoon begin to run down into holiness, aiming the laser beam on her cornea, goofy disease, presumably the reaction of the body to a fungus generated by leaves, earth, dog-shit...so that the eye began to devour itself. She was lucky, if the lesion had ruptured and bled into the eye, at least at the present state of the art, she would have gone blind.

Carefully focused and then let it go.

Perfect.

"Okay....that's it!"

His wife's hands over candles, welcoming the Shabbath Bride, dinner at home and then The Temple where he was president, and sat up on the bima/altar with the Cantor and the Rabbi.

"I want you back here within, let's say, three weeks. I want to monitor this thing carefully. This may be the end of it, or just the beginning..."

Opening the blinds, the sun a red wafer in the late afternoon sky, almost touching the horizon.

"So good luck," he said to Mrs. Wasserman, shook hands, as she went out into the waiting room to pay. Her husband on the faculty (School of Veterinary Medicine) over at State. Good insurance. He was always exalted when he saw that people were taken care of and grieved when he saw they weren't.

Taking off his white coat, last patient and turning to his nurse, "Well, that's it until Monday. It's been a good week, thanks," and he shook her hand, too and went out the back door in the office-complex, down a back set of stairs into the parking lot.

A little guy. You'd lose him in a crowd. Looked like he could be selling insurance or jewelry or stocks or was teaching Russian (he could, both his mother and father spoke it to him since the time he was born) or might even be the swimming coach in the local high school or the local druggist.

Driving home, the music beginning inside him, the Cantor in New York at a Cantor's convention, and the Rabbi had asked him to take over his part both tonight and the next morning.

A blue Chrysler and a white house, a nicely-rounded wife, a scale (25 to 5) of children, six of them...

Twenty minutes before sundown.

He looked at the sky as he came into the house. It was more like the New Mexico desert than Michigan. All the familiar smells, the hallah loaves on the table.

Rivka comes out of the kitchen and kisses him, a look of expectation, hesitancy on her face.

"We might as well begin now!"

And she rounds the kids up....holiness should surround you in all you do, he thinks, as they come noisily into the dining room, you should bind the words of god on our arms and put them on your forehead and put them on our doorways but Shabbat, the sun sliding over the horizon and you slide too, over the waters of holiness into exaltation....

Rivka lights the candles, the words begin, Baruch ata Adonai/ Holy art Thou, God....flowing out of him, this other non-present essential Self that knew that the Dayself was sham, that he was one of the Holy People whose days should have been, were, bounded and enclosed by prayer, as should be the congregation that he was president of, even follow the ancient rules that no one should drive or put on even car-lights as the sun went down. It should all be here until the next morning, you live by the Temple because the Temple is the Center...midrah...he could get lost in the worlds and the melodies of the ceremonial language of God, and he was like a snake shedding its old skin and becoming new every week as he emerged, fresh and glistening, went over to the Temple and sat on the bima during the services while the Cantor sang and he was a kind of silent witness, symbol. But tonight it was different, and then the next morning as he went over to what he always laughingly referred to as the Old Man's Club, as close "essence" as it got in this Reformed-Conservative congregation, with his prayer-shawl around his shoulders, his yarmulke on his head. Sol there, 95, two wives already dead, and he didn't leave the retirement home except to come to Saturday morning temple, and Jake Minsky, who ran a wholesale produce place in Lansing, Ben Kruchkow, the retired history professor, all nine or ten or twelve of them, two or three women, but mainly the old men, pushing the Big Historical Clock back, back before Holocausts and Diasporas, back into the desert just after the Great Revelation on Sinai when Moses came down with his face "scorched," and he had to cover it...came down with the Laws that separated Barbarism from Civilization.

He loved the music that he didn't so much even think of as music but as a necessary way to clothe and decorate the words, the way the 14th century artist-scribe had decorated Asher Ben Jehiel's commentary on the Mishnah by filling the letters with eagles and unicorns, dogs, lions and castles. Or how another illuminator from Spain had turned Hebrew letters into animals themselves so that ALEPH became a horse and a rider....

There could never be too much illumination and embellishment. At heart he was a kaballisti who, like Shem Tov the Sephardi, Isaac of Akko and other "tzerufs," believed that through meditations on the Hebrew alphabet itself, you came into as much oneness as you could with God....

"Shabbat Shalom "

He was sitting there, he was listening, he was THERE, but it took Rivka's shaking him ("Are you okay, Solly, are you okay?") to get him out of the well of his selfness into the rom of candles and armos and love.

"I'm find, just tinking," he said as his children crowded

around him (all but Dave who -- of all things -- had a date with an Irish girl to study for an economics exam on Monday) and he gathered them close to him, murmuring to himself almost as if it weren't a prayer at all YESHIMEHA ELOHIM KEFRAIM VEHEEMNASHAY...peace, sanctification....and then is own personal addition in his heart of hearts...and may these rites and rituals and those who perform them never, never, never be absent from this sad,drunk (Le Bateau Ivre) Earth...

"I want to die in six months, period!"

"You need counseling."

"I need a new back, new legs, new ribs, maybe opium, or even better, a glass of arsenic..."

"Thelma!" Marin started in on her, "Helomut's here for diner, not theater."

"Where did he ever get a name like Helmut? That's like calling someone Gloves or Belt."

"Someone ought to give you a little belt...ing," Martin said, got up and got a new bottle of Cabernet Sauvignon and deftly corkscrewed it open, refilled Helmut's glass.

"Such a beautiful house," gloated Helmet, first taking a scrumptious sip, then getting up and going over to the huge window looking down at the gigantic pink hibuscused and Japanese mapled gardens, to the huge cat-tailed pond with its fountain in the middle, two deer over on the far edge looking at him and the house.

"Look, a mother and her doe."

Martin got up and joined him.

"Beautiful, aren't they! They're always around. I call the mother Rachael and the doe Sarah, the father is Aaron. He comes around a lot, too. What I can't understand is why they let anyone kill deer, or anything else as far as that goes. We're invaders into their sacred territory," then laughing a cynical, guttural laugh, "territory A versus territory B, accent A versus accent B, your God has horns and mine a beard. When I was in the army in India and Persia...oops, Iran...the Dravidians and the Parsi-speakers...like reliving the bible, a thousand little kingdoms, I almost left Judaism and became a Buddhist. Like remember the last chief Buddhist saying, when he was dying, that he'd stop his body from having rigor mortis...and he never had it..."

"What? Rigor what?" Thelma screamed-asking.

"Turn on your hearing aid!"growled Martin, but a beneficent growl, a growl that said, "I love, whatever way it may go, I will always love you."

Five kids.

Two of them dead in plane crashes. Their own private planes, always money, good jobs, imitating Pere Graustein....

Helmut turning away from the window and looking at the photos on the walls, Thelma when she was young, a young Cleopatra, a young Eve making everywhere she went into a garden of paradise.

"You were always so beautiful!"

"Still is," smiles Martin, "whenever I look at her-her, I see the essential her-her..."

"You're sounding philosophical. Jungian!" smiled Helmut.

"Why not?"

"Youngian what?" squirrel-noses Thelma.

"You'll always be young!" Martin still smiling.

"Just hang on to life, that's all," Helmut insisting, feeling inside him all sorts of squirts and shacks of desire for the young beauty in those almost ancient photos, "Believe me, I can be paralyzed in bed, eating, drinking and just seeing and I'll have old Humphrey Bogart films on all day, and Agnes Varda, and what's her name, in Les Parapluies de Cherbourg...?"

"Catherine Deneuve," says Thelma footnote-ishly, like an internet file.

"How did you know that?' Martin overwhelmingly impressed, turning to Helmet, "Is she right?"

"A hundred percent. And I'm only 74 and my memory's like shredded carrots, purple cole slaw. I spend half the night every night trying to remember the names of old friends, professors, girlfriends, books, operas, places...like enghein."

"Where Monet lived before he died," says Thelma flatly.

Martin again overwhelmed with surprise.

"How do you know that? How did you hear that? I thought you're mainly deaf."

"Maybe I can just hear what I want to hear and remember what I want to remember."

"What she should have done is been an art history professor, something like that, art history, film history..."

"Instead of being his Brunhilde," Thelma really laughing now, poking Martin in the ribs, "I can practically hear the music," stop as if she were listening to hordes of musicians and singers inside the concert hall of her memory.

"What music?" Martin, the ex-soldier/cavalier, 85.3% outside of everything 'high cultural.'

"Wagner. The Ring Operas. We should start watching opera every night. DVD's with subtitles no less, and French films like Les Laisons Dangereux, Les Parapluies de Cherbouerg....go to Prague, Budapest..goulash...Spanish tapas..."

Martin suddenly with tears in his eyes, half-whispering to Helmet, "She hasn't grabbed on to life like this for decades," then turning to her, louder, "Okay, whatever you say..."

"You can't feel back-pain when you're killing dragons or chasing after gods and goddesses. I love the new part of the Louvre."

"The Jewish museum in Prague. A little depressing, but...."

"My house-contractor father who always wanted to be a painter, filling the walls of our houses...houses...one in Boston, the other on Martha's Vineyard, filling all the walls with Frenchish impressionistic paintings."

Martin getting all turned on.

"You should have seen the synagogues in India. All over the place. Beautiful. And I love Notre Dame in Paris, that little church on the Isle San Louis."

She walks over to the huge TV in the corner and grabs the controller, takes the DVD out of a little box on the table next to it, DVD on, open, ein, zwei, drei, titles in English and a little jumping ahead and there's Siegfried vouching for, screaming about, singing about his eternal love of
Brunhilde.

Too loud, but...

"That's what I want for me," grabbing her arms around midgetish, almost frail Martin.

"Me too," he agrees and crushes her back, Helmet expecting a back-pain scream, but instead her face turns into pure bliss satori, "I'm so tired of the real world and real people, I want to swim all day and night in an art-world..."

"That I'm in too?" Martin feigning a little worry.

"Of course...and you too Helmet...at least part time."

As Brunhilde, warrior-woman rather quickly turns into an eternal Mother Earth-Wind-Sky.

DAS HELDENLEBEN/THE HERO'S LIFE

His intensions were...what were they really? He hadn't seen her for 50 years, had gotten her married name from a mutual friend, a grammar school pal he'd been pals with for 68 years!.

Deutsch, Karen Deutsch. She was German, Gretta Hapsburg, but to have married someone named Deutsch?!?!? He was going to be down in Chicago for this huge ophthalmologist convention, Soxtember, the White Sox world Series madness every, every, everywhere, had called her from Ann Arbor a week before the convention.

"Maybe we could meet for coffee, whatever, at Borders on Michigan Avenue, you know, by Loyola..."

"I don't know," she hesitated. After all he had dumped her, she hadn't dumped him, 50 years earlier. "Do you really think...?"

He filled in the blanks.

"Should, might, can, ought to, can handle it? Why not? There weren't two people in the world closer than us..."

"Fifty years ago, mais...okay, Friday morning 10 o'clock, Borders on Michigan Avenue by the Water Tower..."

Hung up, feeling dejected, wanted to keep talking, cajoling, teasing her over the phone. Fifty years. And the way they'd broken up had been so idiotic. Idiotic him, Mr. Daily Communion, the body and blood of Christ, the real presence, the Flesh albigensionishly evil, sex only for one thing, procreation, if you had fun, that was only incidental, and outside the procreation wire, it was the deepest, darkest sin....

They'd been at La Petite Gourmet on Michigan Avenue, this fancy restaurant in the Italian Court, now replaced by another building, but in the old days almost a real Italian court, balconied apartments surrounding a fountain-centered courtyard.

The pianist in the background playing the laziest, lolling, almost-jazz, almost Debussyian music, both of them sucking on whiskey sours, him admiring the engagement ring on her finger, for which she'd supplied the diamond and he (his mother) the magnificent gold setting.

And suddenly she gets very serious-solemn, takes his hand. She's a beautiful piece of a woman, looking very Parisian, Parisian modelish, all the right shoes, dress, hat, just a touch of a black veil, like just off the cover of Vogue.

"I've got something serious to tell you, something I, in all honesty, have to tell you...remember last summer, when I worked on Cape Cod? Well, I met this Harvard guy. We worked in the same restaurant together, and every night we'd go off to the beach, and...," she hesitates, this is a confession from the heart of puritanical Catholicism, "we'd have sex every night on the beach. No one ever saw us, 'caught' us, the beach was always totally deserted..."

She stops. His face is suddenly angry granite and he gets abruptly up, talking loud enough for everyone in the restaurant to hear. None of her whisperings for him.

"Okay, take a good look, because this is the last time you're ever going to see this face."

Standing like he was posing for a snapshot. One, two, three, snap, and then out the door as she begins to inaudibly cry, the most poignant kind of crying, totally wrapped up in herself, and a grief that's more like funereal than something to do with a broken engagement.

Out he goes, 5,4,3,2,1, and then a sudden turn, return, back to the table.

"Come on, I'll drive you home, I can't leave you down here alone at this time of night."

And she gets up all mute and humblized now, her whiplash wild-woman self gone and replaced by a mourner for her own life.

Out to his father's black Chevy, all the way home no talk, and when he drops her off at her (her parents' place) no kiss, no more words, although both of them wanted to talk.

It had really been spilled all over them all their lives and then crystallized in their dreams: THE FLESH IS EVIL, THE SPIRIT IS GOOD, SO FOLLOW THE SPIRIT WHEREVER IT TAKES YOU, AND YOU'LL END UP FOREVER IN A SEXLESS HEAVEN WITH CLOUDS, ANGELS, THE RESURRECTED CHRIST, THE BLESSED VIRGIN, ST. JOSEPH, THE SAINTS AND ALL THE SAVED. The flesh had only one purpose-- reproduction. Any pleasure was just a by-product, not the real point.

He pulled over to the curb in front of her house. Both fighting not to talk, love still there like moonlight spread all over them, but no goodbyes, she just got out and went inside without looking back, he still admiring her legs, lusting after her legs in the streetlight...and then she was gone.

Fifty years. He got to Borders an hour early, had a cinnamon roll that they stuck in the microwave and half melted. Delicious, almost burned his tongue. No knives or forks for him, just delicious gummy hands. No coffee, him and his sleep problems, just milk. Perfect. Parfait. Looked out at the old water tower, the new water-tower mall, his alma mater, Loyola...felt 100% at home.

Had brought the Penguin book of French verse and was reading some Baudelaire without translation, doing very well, when, 9:55, there she was getting in line at the coffee shop.

That was her, wasn't it, this old lady with long white hair tied up on top of her head, glasses, a cane...?

He got up and came over to her.

"You are you, aren't you?"

"Just an old house that needs rebuilding..."

"Don't we all."

"You look fine...better than fine, belle..."

"I wouldn't go that far."

"I would."

And suddenly Boarders Books tearoom began to turn green for him, turn into Lincoln Park or down around the University of Chicago, Loyola's Lake Shore Campus, Ravinia...all the places they used to go, all the concerts and exhibits at the Art Institute, or just fooling around, parks or in his (his father's) car when he took her home, not just lust, though, which was always the big taboo, but they'd both read Aldous Huxley's Point Counter Point and they'd go see Pride and Prejudice or Clouzot's Le Corbeau or Jules and Jim, go to Le Petite Gourmet Cafe and when he walked in his pianist pal would stop whatever she was playing and, for a few minutes, play Debussy's "Maid with the Flaxen Hair," which always made him and Karen feel like royalty....

"We always read the same books, remember, Waugh, Huxley, Virginia Woolf, Borges...?" tears in his eyes. Taking her hands.

Her, almost crying, too.

"I'd better get going..."

"You can't just give into your feelings? You're obviously feeling the same thing that I'm feeling..."

"But I'm not you, am I?"

Getting up with difficulty, he wanted to stop her, kidnap her, take her to some imaginary castle on Lake Delevan in Wisconsin, to a chateau he didn't have but wished he had in the Loire Valley, or a place somewhere on the island of Santa Catarina in Brazil, anywhere, everywhere, another couple of thousand years with her, to Valhalla to get some of Freya's Apples of Immortality, and never-ever die...

"Au revoir," she half-choked out and as he got up she took him in her arms and open-mouth kissed him, tasting of cinnamon and sugar, obviously didn't want to let go, but did, turned slowly, obviously going against everything she deep-down felt, and slowly walked out of the coffee shop to the bookstore, to the escalator, and was gone.

He wanted to follow after her, could have easily caught up with her. But what did he ultimately want, to leave his third wife from Provençal and give up their yearly trips to France? Besides, his French wife was pure beauty and empathy too, n'est pas?

So he sat, thinking about Gretta's Michigan Avenue apartment, the Chicago symphony, the Art Institute, Roosevelt University's music and drama department...

"Forget it!"

But he'd write. He wanted to at least bond with her spiritually, hated the idea that they'd both be under gravestones in just a few years. At best.

CHARLEMAGNE PIGEON

The law finally got passed in the Michigan legislature:

WE HEREBY DECREE THAT FROM THIS
TIME FORWARD IT SHALL BE 100%
LEGAL TO HUNT PIGEONS, NOT ONLY
DURING THE REGULAR HUNTING SEASON
BUT ALL YEAR LONG.

Charley Pigeon out by the Looking Glass River in Holt, flying around as usual with his girl-friend, Muriel, the cutest pigeon in the world, this guy in a hunting jacket walking along with a gun in his hand. No need to worry, they're not deer, bears, partridges, pheasants, porcupines, wolves...pigeons are exempt from death...he thinks...until the guy lifts his rifle up to his shoulder, and BAM! Muriel is dead next to him.

"Holy Crow, let me outta here!"

The hunter raising his gun again, Charlemagne suddenly flying into the pine trees as fast as he can, the bullet/bullets whizzing past his ears, finds a quiet, shady place on a branch, a place where he's invisible, waits until the hunter goes by and then begins to quietly weep--weep-weep, beep-beep, cry.

The hunter walks away and is gone for a while, but then, when he comes back, he has a radio on, the news, and Charlemagne hears the impossible, the legislature has passed a law that it's legal to kill PIGEONS.

Really mad now, his feathers all erect in anger, looking like a walking pin-feather cushion.

"I'll show um...," thinking back to his ancestors millions of years back, prehistoric pigeon dinosaurs the size of banks, the Eiffel towers, fighting with rhinos and Rex Tyrannosaurses...

"What I need is armor! What we need is organization!"

And he starts flying through the woods, over the fields, over the ponds and rivers, pigeon-screaming out the best he can, "Fellow pigeons, meet in the stadium at Michigan State University, no game today, they're playing the University of Siberia in Siberia, meet me in the stadium, I have something really important to tell you..."

He was so effective that not only did hundreds of pigeons come to the stadium, but scores of ducks, sparrows, even some dragon-flies...

And once they had filled the stadium up, well, filled one-tenth of it, Charlemagne got down in the middle of the field with a morning glory megaphone and started speaking/twittering:

"Fellow pigeons and other bird-kin, we're going to have to take over and dominate the human world, or else humans are going to destroy us. There's a new law that allows pigeon-hunting...as if they hadn't killed pigeons before. So in order to survive, quite simply we have to TAKE OVER!!"

A claw went up, an Egret.

"Only bladablablabla?"

"I can't quite make out what you're saying."

That strong Egret accent. Almost impossible to understand.

"If we bladablla can't even blaa blaa talk and be...bladedbla understood...how can we bladeblabla take over any blada anything?"

Ah, he finally got it!

"Hypnotism!"he answered, "my Czech pigeon grandmother taught me a way to coo-boo, boo-hoo that hypnotizes human beings and makes them do whatever I want them to do. Come on, I'll show you!"

And off he goes, all the other birds following him, files downtown, out of the forest to the state capital, the Senate and House of Representatives being talked to by the governor, this redhead with a face full of pimples, but still a knockout.

All the birds try to get through the revolving door, this one lawyer seeing them, laughing like crazy.

"Man, here comes Christmas', New Year's and Fourth of the July's dinners!"

"Watch me!" Charlemagne beeps to the other birds and starts to coo hypnotically, the lawyer who'd been laughing at all the birds suddenly straightening up , eyes glazed,
totally and stiffly hypnotized.

"Yes, what can I do for you, master?"

"Take me into the state Senate and House of Representatives so I can do my stuff."

"So we can do our stuff," coos Peter Pigeon, a friend of Charlemagne.

"Okay....here we go," and the lawyer swings open the door of the two chambers, with the governor sitting up in the power position on the bench, the whole huge room filled with senators and house of representative people, as Charlemagne begins his hypnotic cooing, at first everyone pooh-poohing him, "What's that bird doing in here anyhow, him and his pals?," one senator even going so far as to scream at him, "I thought they were supposed to kill off all you guys by now," Charlemagne giving the signal to the rest of the birds, "Imitate me, you can learn," and they all begin, at first comically ineffective, all the guys and gals laughing at them, throwing pencils and crumpled paper balls at them, and then slowly coming under the magic spell, the governor eventually asking, all hypnotized and tamed, "What can I do for you, oh Masters of the Universe?"

"Out of here, all of you, we're taking over!"

""But what about elections?" one of the senators complains.

"You're electing us right now. Does that make sense?"

"Of course, of course."

And they leave, all the pigeons and other birds take their

seats and Charlemagne takes a gravel in his mouth and bangs on the top of his desk, at the same time squeaking out, "Okay, everyone, time to come to order, time to come to order, I'd like to start with proposing a law that we can shoot Senators and Congressmen. All in favor, coo 'Yeah.'"

A lot of cooing, almost 100% in favor, one white crane with long yellow legs complaining, "Why imitate evil, why not find our own way, our own path?"

"Overruled, my friend," answered Charlemagne, and the law was passed.

Suddenly there was a loud knock on the door. The president of the senate, John D. Dooley MFA (in sculpture), "Listen, me and my colleagues have been talking about the present situation and have decided to become pigeons, too. Costumes, Okay, but aren't suits and ties costumes? What do you think?"

Charlemagne invites him in, to sit in the back while he puts it to a vote.

"All in favor of letting the gringos become pigeons and cancelling the killer-senator law, coo YEAH!"

All kind of cooing, very vigorous.

"Okay, obviously the yes-es have won," turning to Dooley, "One week to get pigeonized, Okay?"

"OKAY, your highness," and out they go and announce to the Senators and Congressmen, "Okay, my friends, it's a pigeon-world from now on, everyone gets pigeonized or else it's a Holy War against the featherless-beakless..."

Everyone cheers.

Terrorism has been conquered.

One year later.

We walk down to Old Town by the Fluvial River; cars pass us by, everyone driving wearing pigeon-masks, one guy down by the river fishing, Mr. Pigeon-Face. It's five o'clock, all the pigeon-people are coming out of their offices, we move to the Capital, into the Senate/House of Representatives, a medical expert up in front of them explaining "We're very seriously working on getting to the point where we can turn people into pigeons, pigeons into people, or at least arrive at a half-way point -- pigemans!"

Cheer-coos from everyone.

Everything has been settled, end of terrorism, peace forever in the offing.

Then suddenly the back door is kicked open, everyone turns. What now?

It's a wolf on a horse.

A shudder of fear passes across everyone. Wolves eat pigeons, n'est pas?

"Okay, all you guys and gals and our coo-coo brothers are fine. But what about us? And porcupines, walruses, badgers, llamas...you know...what about US?"

"Here's something I came across in the basement yesterday," Jean had told her daughter, Suzie, the day before, as they were sitting in the dining room of Jean's just-dead (one week) ninety-five year old father. She had inherited the house and all its contents. Her sister, Martha, had inherited the other house in Cádiz, which had made Martha very happy...a place to spend her winters in, away from Kansas City. But Jean was very happy with the house in Michigan because her father had only spent ten years of winters in Spain and fifty years all year around there (minus the Spanish winters), and it held most of his "serious" belongings in it, including the family silver.

But Jean had already told Martha that she'd share the more "serious" stuff with her, which, to Martha, meant silver, paintings, jewelry, whatever could be re-sold for quick cash. Which was what Martha was mainly concerned with.

Jean, though, especially wanted the books and manuscripts, the books her father had written, the signed poems from other poets (and himself) all over the walls, the endless copies of signed small editions of now dead "small-press" poets who were slowly assuming classic dimensions. Martha and Jean differed radically on how they regarded their father's poetry and the poetry of his "circle," what he had always called his "gang." Martha thought of it all as ephemera, but Jean saw it as the work of Rimbauds, Hart Cranes, Verlaines, Kafkas, Apollinaires...regarded her father, especially, as a kind of latter day Rimbaud.

Suzie was rather tentative about the old notebook. Perfect bound. Black. A sketch-book, notebook, really. Her grandfather hadn't ever wanted to write in anything with lines. It made him feel "constrained," "Tied-down," "controlled."

Her mother wouldn't be back to the old house for another

few hours, some problems with the restaurant. One of the chefs had been or was going to be deported back to Mexico. The best "French" cook she'd had for years. But she was certain something could be done, had her lawyer in on it. Lawyer and old friend, "That's the way it should always be. Business should never be separated from pleasure, everything should always be seamless, one piece..."

Suzie was supposed to keep poking and sorting things, she supposed, but instead drifted out into the garden and found one of her grandfather's old, many-times-painted fan-backed wooden chairs under an ancient oak, opened the notebook cautiously and began to read:

> I'm beginning to write this on the day of your birth, January 3rd, 1967. Cold every place but here in Cadíz. I talked to your mother on the phone this morning, our morning, her midnight. Said she couldn't sleep: "Against all sense and logic and power of biochemistry, I am wide awake, and it's a girl. I like the name Susan, don't you? Like 'Black-Eyed Susans,' 'Oh, Susannah, don't you cry for me...' Oh, I feel so overwhelmingly silly. I guess I was supposed to go into post-partum depression or something, but I've never felt so high."
>
> Good sign. Good omen. You come on the scene like a sunrise.
>
> What I'm going to try to do here is -- ha, ha -- give you the accumulated wisdom of my long years as itinerant philosopher, poet, mythologist, anthropologist, whatever you want to call me.
>
> I was reading Mary Shelley's Frankenstein today and as I read through it, page after page of Dr. Frankenstein's travels, I thought that's what I

should tell you, "Travel, travel, travel, go to England and Scotland, the Lake District, the moors, over to the Dordogne, the Alps, go to Prague and Vienna, learn the languages, find strange alleys and strange allies, make strange alliances and have strange loves, grasp it all to you like a cloak of rose petals....or even, when it hurts, like a cloak of thorns. Why such a concentration on The Strange? Well, then I thought exactly the opposite, never leave your village of Winona Point, Wisconsin, get married and mother ten children, end up with a hundred grandchildren, end up matriarchal beyond belief, creatrix of your own private race/tribe.

Six generations down and they'll number a million, if they all keep up your pace. But one thing you'll never suffer from is what I have most suffered from -- a sense of unreality, isolation, getting up in the morning and reaching out and being surprised when I can actually feel/grasp a glass of milk, actually open a door instead of floating through it. One husband, stability, friends, a whole town that knows you....isn't that one way of answering the unanswerable?

And forget about One God way Out There someplace in Never-Never-Land. The ancients were right where the moderns are wrong. Religion has been very wrong for the last few thousand years. Listen to the river gods and the forest gods, the cloud and rain gods and goddesses...go out into the forest away from Man and feel the presences. And don't try to figure it all out logically. Imagine you're a red corpuscle in someone's bloodstream and you suddenly become "conscious." What could you know? That there were moments of aeration and depletion, contractile movements...maybe you could figure out you were in some sort of stream and there was a pump, a "rich" area, "poor" area...you were mortal...but could you ever figure out you were in somebody's body, much less figure out that the body was in a room and that the room was in a house, the house was on the surface of a planet, and there were a sun and moon, planets, stairs...well, we're like that, no idea what is beyond our closed system. In whose veins are we circulating? What is beyond the walls of our cosmic arteries?

One thing for sure, there is one master-message being beamed at us full time. Think of all the eggs that your ovaries are going to produce during your lifetime. Think of all the sperms produced by your husband or husbands, lover/lovers. Think of all the seeds of all the trees produced in Spring, all the beans and peas and seeds-in watermelons, squash, pumpkins. The message is pretty obvious.

THE CORE OF EVERYTHING IS LIFE, REPRODUCTION. What is all this nonsense about unmarried priests, celibate "sisters"? The last thing that God wants/the Gods want, is celibacy. Nature is profligate, it calls for profligacy. Everything screams L'CHAIM, L'CHAIM, L'CHAIM, TO LIFE, TO LIFE, TO LIFE!!! And shouldn't that same sort of generosity extend out to everything?

I mean enthusiasm. Invent God/Gods! God has me in his hands in the morning and in the afternoon. He brings on the dawn and the dusk, he holds all the living and dead in his power. Why hold back? Your breasts and vagina and legs, hair, skin....rush to meet Life, don't hold back and treat life as if it were an enemy. The ducks descend, snow, rain, leaves, death....so it's late Winter, say, you're walking along beside the Red Cedar River, it's cold, snowy, cloudy, whatever it is, you're not projecting out to somewhere else or into some other time that's already been or is going to be, you're entirely there, this is it, nothing else has ever been or will be, your skin is there, your eyes, your smell, taste, ears, every fir tree, Dawn Redwood, Tamarack, Chinese Tree of Heaven, every face that passes you or you pass, the movement of the water under the ice, the movement of clouds over, under and around the sun...if you grasp it all to you in all the dimensions of its clarity, you can die with a sense of enough, ça sufit, surfeit, the feast ends, but at least it was a feast....

She stopped. There wasn't much more anyhow, just a few more pages.

But really couldn't go on, wasn't sure exactly what she felt, a strange mixture of awe, a sense that she was very personally, almost nastily, being censored, a certain repugnance at, what would you call it, "vulgarity," and, more than anything else, a sense that under all the flourishes and fanfares, he was essentially right, IT was there right outside the window, Spring, Summer, Fall, Winter, always on the edge of making "Itself" visible, and in a sense always did, in all the things that simply happened...like the rain just beginning again now, on the edge of Spring, a week before Easter, snow-god, rain-god, spring-god, feeling infinitely sad that the grand old man had died, after ten impossible years in coma, six years before that vague and only fragmentarily "there" at all, before he'd really ever had anything but the slightest sense of who he had been writing to, way back when, twenty years before, when she had been born...

GAMES

They'd both been published in the same magazine, Dandelion Dust, and both their poems were so close to each other it was scary. Even the same titles: "Ghosts."

GHOSTS (His)
Everyone a ghost now,
all my old beer -- and bowling--
pals, Okinawa and Red Soxes
versus White Soxes, old girlfriends
becoming tombstones, you
reach out to touch long black hair
and you touch stone.

GHOSTS (Hers)
I'm a ghost, you're a ghost,
who's the tastiest, ghostiest
ghost-dog in our Comisky Park
dreams,
tums, tumble, tombs,
three "T's,"
GUTT
BYE.

He saw himself as Mr. Serious Poet, a modern-day Rilke, but he wrote her anyhow, got her address from the editor of Tomato Ketchup, where she published a lot. She had gotten him, Mr. Grim Guts, to smile, hadn't she? That was a major feat in itself, wasn't it?

Dear Frau Muller:
Loved your poem in the latest issue of
Tomato Ketchup,one of the few do-it-as-
thou-willst mags still left in down-the-slide
Gringolandia, and I thought maybe we
could strike up an e-mail friendship, my e-
mail is Samstump@ABC.com.
Sending along another book of mine from a
few years back, Soul Grub. Just for fun. I'd
like to get some idea of what you look like,
how about a picture?

And off it went with his Saturday morning mailings of
poems, stories, articles plays, always used the post-office at
Michigan State in the Student Union, no lines; where he had taught
literary nonsense for forty years.

Trouble getting up the steps now. Allein, allein, allein, but
he loved Michigan, the endless farms, forests, deer, ducks, drakes,
lakes, lagoons, even snakes, porcupines, black bears, go out any
direction, N.S.E. or West from the center of downtown East
Lansing and you'd be in sister landscapes of Bavaria, Ireland,
Southern France, one vast impressionistic painting.

One week later a picture arriving, two pictures, one of the
gypsy-black-eyed Vamp with anthracite coal-black hair and a look
on her face that said "Whatever you want, I can double," and two
pictures of her, what, thirty(?), forty (?), fifty (?) years later, alt/ old,
yes, but not all that old either, and still the Pigalle street-bunny in
her eyes as she sat in front of a huge white frosted birthday cake
that looked like a wedding cake (or was it a funeral cake?), and
another photo of her watering palms in a living room someplace
next to long, dark drapes, black and white too.

"Here they are!" the note said, "Where are yours?" And then
signed "Gypsy Strummings, Angel-Eyes."

Very nice. He was always so curious about gypsies, the wild ones, clicking heels and lifted skirts, blackbird eyes and ketchup lips, iceberg teeth, "Was willst du mit mir? Alles ! / What do you want from me? Everything!"

Went into the cabinet next to his bed for some pictures of himself and found two from Madrid, sitting on a bench in front of an ancient Egyptian temple the Egyptians had given the Spanish when they were fooling around with the Nile and had to get the temple out of the way.

Just a few years back, after his wife had died from diabetes/cancer. He'd taken

off "To Hell and back," or maybe never back, enough money to stay in whatever Heaven, Hell, Purgatory he might find, her money his money, back to Spain or Oberammergau, Ghent, Amsterdam, him fat and smiling and looking younger as he travelled. Mr. Zest, in the middle of the quest. For what? And then always back to magic Michigan. Hearing gypsy violins in his head as he put the photos in an envelope. Media mail. Good enough. He'd mail them Saturday morning with the rest of his poem- and story-submissions.

Wiedersehen, meine geliebte, bis..../ Seeya later, sweetheart, until....

Dropped a little note inside the envelope with the photos.

Time to sleep. And, brother, was he tired. Satisfied, fulfilled, like he'd had an orgasm and a swing of Nyquil, ten years since castration for prostate cancer, sex like something from a previous incarnation.

II

Every morning he began his day with e-mails to his poet-friends in Deutschland, NY, Walla Walla, Washington, San

Francisco....and now L.A.

> Dear Angela,
> How dem nippie-whippies doin'? Can't ya-al
> send me a DVD of you gypsy-stripping in the
> park in the dark maybe with just a little
> candlelight to make it right, all them sensuous
> body-landscapes moving to the tune of music
> wrestling.
> I can't wait to meet you. Maybe we can get
> together at Harvard where my daughter
> Elizabeth (I always calledher Queen Elizabeth)
> teaches.
> Or I can come to California and we can bum
> around in downtown L.A., the Central Market,
> Chinatown, go down to Venice and sit with all
> the other old Jews looking at the surf...maybe
> find a Japanese restaurant and eat some
> ginger...
>
> Love, Kisses and Whatever Else,
> Heinrich Flugelhorn

Sent it, within hours had an answer:

> Loved your letter, only my husband saw it too,
> very jealous, he's Siciliano, maybe six months to
> live, intestinal cancer and all that, but you never
> know, maybe I should sleep in the garage,
> padlock the door shut, but then he could always
> pour gasoline all around it and set it on fire,
> block my getting out...let's keep the letters a little

more "professional," literary...who are your
favorite contemporary poets? Who has been
the biggest influence on your own work? More
samples of your work. Maybe some books in
the mail, "corrections"/"suggestions" viz a viz
my work...you see where I'm going, n'est pas,
away from the groin and into the
BRAIN/SENSIBILITIES, not sensualities...Okay?

Which gave him a kick. Like his Manichee-Albigensian-
Cathar childhood in Albania, sex is evil, we are here to die, no
other reason, the only hope is the next life, this life is minus
infinity....waited a couple of days, just to get her anxious and then:

Dear Angel-Ass,
Loved your descriptions of your maxi-duro-
orgasms that you have alone now that your
husband's heart problems prevent him from
being active sexually. We'll get together soon,
like you said. Tell him you're visiting some
editor somewhere, editor, writers' workshop,
some old friend from college, and I'll meet you
in Cincinnati or Somerville, Massachusetts,
Kansas City, you can even come here, lots of
room just waiting to be filled by secretary you,
you of the door-bell nipples. Love your nipple-
centrism.
You don't talk about me in your sleep, do you,
oh, baby, more, more, more...what we do we
do, baby-boobies, isn't adultery but psycho-
physical therapy, Zen sanity, a walk through
psychosomatic beatitude...
                    Kisses and Climaxes.

And off the letter went.

He waited for a response that afternoon, evening, the next morning, finally, chewing on 500 mg. chewable vitamin C's (4 of them) he wrote her:

What's wrong? Are you okay? Don't get me all worried.

Still no response He'd write a little, every morning, as if everything were okay, How's your pomegranates, Miss your grapefruits and watermelon (ass)...what's wrong?, what's wrong? Wrongdoing, no dong-doing.....

The letters kept getting sillier and sillier, shorter and shorter, until finally, like a cured alcoholic, taking one swig of Irish Crème liquor every morning after breakfast, he'd manage one word a day:

LOVE.

That was it. And then she changed her e-mail company and he had no e-mail address for her, phone-number changed too, no longer listed. Silence. His days becoming like a morgue, feeling cadaverous, thinking about death all day and all night, would it be heart, bowel cancer, a recurrence of prostate cancer, a car accident...even suicide?

III

Six months pass. He's on his computer as usual one morning, reading some "shards" from his poet-friend, John Bennett, a kind of non-poetic/post-poetic poetry that Bennett sent every-every-every day, a letter from Blythe Ayne, a genius-friend in Washougal, Washington....and there was a strange e-mail address he didn't recognize: Zany@aol.com, clicked on it, it was Angel:

My husband has been dead for three months now. I've been going to his grave every day, sitting there as if waiting for his soul/ghost to come back, like that old Frankenstein-resurrected film I saw when I was a kid. Why don't you come and visit. Get the tickets and I'll pick you up at the airport. Wear a red cap so I'll recognize you. I'm sure all the photos you sent me were from twenty years back. Just give me the day, flight number, arrival time, and I'll do all the rest....

Love (or something very like it),
Gypsy Angel

Which deeply touched him. Alone for so many years, his kids in China, Boston, Brazil, Vietnam (teaching piano)...and now suddenly a YEA!, in the midst of a thousand-thousand silent NEH's!

The next day he went to the You Wanit, We Gotit travel agency in town and got a ONE WAY ticket to L.A. via Chicago, wanted to get it for the next day, but the best he could do was two weeks, e-mailed La Gitana that night, she-e-mailed him back "Okay!," and then "Over and Out." He'd arrive in L.A. the first Sunday in September, still filled with vague memories, like scars, about September = Classes Re-begin. Took one of his favorite old light grey caps and dyed it red in a sauce pan. Looked good. September. A light tweed jacket, maybe he'd buy a new pipe, wear a normal tweed cap until he got to the L.A. airport and then turn from Old Englisher Sherlock Holmes into Señor Red Cap.

Nervous about seeing her, almost feels like cancelling it , bowing-, chickening-, chicken-shitting-out, but then remembering his old grandmother in her even older rocking chair, "Wir haben nur eine Leben, und leben wir müssen, vor sterben/ We have only one life and live we must...before dying...."

IV

He got off the plane gingerly. If he could have bought tweed bags too, he would have. Too hot in all the tweeds, but IMAGE WAS ALL, if the Queen doesn't look like the queen, she's not the Queen.

Nobody out there waiting for him as he walked down the ramp into the airport, Niemand, niemand, niemand, no one, no one, no one, all ready to go back, find a roof to jump off of, tie a rock around his neck and jump into the Black Bear River, Zeit nach hause zu gehen/ Time to go home....hause/ home...wishing he believed in castles in the afterlife sky where he could spend eternities sipping on Chianti and Irish Creme...wo bist tu, meine Geliebte? / Where are you, my beloved? And then suddenly this angel-trumpet voice, "There you are, my beast! I thought you'd chickened out!"

Just standing there, like he was looking under a microscope at genital warts, or in Florence at the Uffizi Gallery looking at original Leonardos.

"Can't you talk, react? Are you okay?"

She was old, maybe more than he'd expected, but just the kind of old he liked, thin-svelte, sterling silver hair, glasses, all dressed in red with black tights and flat black suede shoes...

"I'm sorry about the shoes, but I can't wear heels..."

"Yes, you can, lying down..."

Which got her heartily laughing.

"Lying down...as in my coffin?"

"Our coffin," he laughed back, thinking of her in bed and him massaging what
he knew had to be her still breathtaking feet and legs, old-lady feet and legs, which made them even more breathtaking, antique. She

was a living antique, the Great Mother/Grandmother incarnate, radiating not just end-of-the-line gorgeousness, but benignity more benign than black cherry jam, the best of possible crêpes, sauerkraut mit brautwurst, the old Jewish museum in Prague...

He held on to her, held, held, held, her finally whispering in his ear, "Do you have to pick up any more luggage, or is this is?"

"It!"

"Can't I...?"

Trying to grab one of the bags.

"No...," following her through the station to the parking ramp, looking at her ankles, feet, he'd brought along all sorts of Patchoulish lotions, feet, legs and up, worship at the altar of her body, post-castrati, cancer-cured, sexless, but....

Feeling all sexed up, at the same time totally aware of the absurdity of such feelings...and sleepy...old...too much travelling, should have gotten some coffee on the plane to snap him back alive again.

Again concentrating very intensely on the driving, off big highways to smaller roads, it had been half a century since he'd been in L.A., his mind flooding with all his dead friends....if he'd only MADE it instead of just brushing with MAKING IT.

Then suddenly....a monster big red truck coming their way on the other side of the street a block down, and she suddenly swerved toward it, the truck-driver started honking, slamming on his brakes, but she kept aiming right at him, then at the last, last moment swerved out of the way, back to normal, no problem with sleepiness now, he was all red-hot peppers and screaming gulls.

"What the fuck was that about?"

Pulling over to the side of the road in front of an old brick apartment house.

"I thought that if I killed us, the two of us together, that we'd be together for all eternity...."

Cried a bit, handkerchief out of her purse, then redoing her eye makeup, him reaching over and kissing her on the lips as she carefully pulled out on the street again, him wondering what Paleolithic cave that theology came out of, die together, together for all eternity...nothing to do with his belief that we're the same as flies, iguanas, apples...to die is to die is to die...die...

CLOUDS

Clouds walked in through the cloudy door wondering what was coming next when suddenly there was his old college buddy, Sam Gazzolo, waiting for him.

"You're looking more like twenty than...how old are you?"

"This is your first day here; you're going to have to learn how to cope."

"With what?"

"Everything."

"But you look twenty, what's the story?"

"Come on in and sit down."

"And your lisp is gone."

"Don't get me mad!"

"I never minded the lisp. But how did you get rid of it."

"It just went away. Like a head cold. Everything bad went away. Dominus Vobiscum, et cum spiritu tuo..."

The richest guy Claude had ever known, never had had to work because his father had owned a drug-company chain in Chicago. Sam's Superdrugs. His son was Sam Jr.

But after his father had died, Sam Jr. had gotten enough money so that he didn't have to not only not work, but could go wherever he wanted whenever he wanted, and the money doubled after his mother died. So all he did was go to church, church, church, hated Vatican II, found a Russian Uniate Church that was Russian, okay, but not orthodox, had never broken its ties with Rome.

So he was like back in the 17th century permanently, a masterpiece house in Oak Park, an English manor that he turned into French, and he never finished college,
just married, travelled to wherever there were great restaurants and nice museums, Florence, Paris, Prague, five kids....

"So how are your kids?"

"Oh, you know, all that travelling, one studied art and is in Milan, none are in the car business, that's great, isn't it?"

"Unless they become Chinese..."

Frank laughs, his old-time silly-boy laugh.

"What a coincidence you should mention China, one is in Taiwan married to a Taiwanese Catholic. Ten kids. Total sanity. What about yours?"

"Six kids, three wives, I've been busy..."

"But divorce isn't allowed in the Church!"

"I've become a Buddhist..."

"A Buddhist, but how did you...?"

(A beautiful young Italian-looking woman walks in, Debussy suddenly in the air, Petite Suite # V).

"I can't believe it!" croaks Claude, "Bella, bella, it's not you is it?! Dolores!"

She embraces him quickly, pulls away when he starts enjoying it a bit too much.

"Still piano-ing?"

He can barely get the words out.

"What else?"

"I thought you had gone into...."

She suddenly gets serious, full of mocking nastiness, "'By the power vested in me...' What about the power of the hands on the keyboard?"

She starts to play an invisible keyboard and we hear Wagner's The Sigfried Idyll
adapted for piano.

"What's that?"

Frank all interested.

"Wagner. Sure, the recitatifs are just talk, but when he comes to melodies, no one can beat him..."

"Except Howard Hansen," adds Sam, "his romantic

symphony is my all-time favorite...."

"My all-time favorite is Vaughan Wllliams' Greensleeves," says Claude a little guiltily.

"Mine is what I'm playing," Dolores, angry, wanting just one thing, to play.

"It's your life, isn't it?" Claude smirks.

"My soul, my spiritual food. I never wanted to be a lawyer, but a musician...in my family it was being a kangaroo, a Mafioso, terrorist...Nazi...that was more like it back then, a Nazi..."

"The world's always been crazy, hasn't it?" Frank, getting very serious, "the Romans and Jesus-Messiah, the Arabs and the Spanish, the Cid, Martin Luther, the Albigensians..."

"Albi...?" asks Dolores, stopping playing a moment.

"The Catholics used to cut up heretics...."

And then she suddenly turned herself off from the rest of the world, shushes everyone, starts playing Debussy's "Maid With the Flaxen Hair."

Claude loved it, her style, her herness, and started wondering about WHO NEXT? Phyllis Miller, one of his friends in pre-med who got killed in a car wreck, and when he went to the funeral and saw her all sewed up in her coffin it was an experience he never got over, voices in him from then on whispering "You're next, no matter how long you have you're still next," suddenly the faces, the music all starting to jiggle and twist and turn around in front of him and in his ears, like he was a potato getting mashed...a voice from Hell stabbing into his world.

"Okay, Claude, c'est temps, it's time."

His wife's voice, it really always was like a medieval fencing sword stuck into the guts of his existentialism.

Eyes opened. There she was, aggressively Brazilian, only he still wasn't quite 100% there.

"I'm supposed to be retired; I can sleep all day if I want."

"More nightmares?"

Ms. Big Psychiatrist. He wanted to tell her to keep her knowhow on the job, not using it in the house, especially not on him.

"Keep this up and you'll spend all day in the mental hospital. What were you nightmaring about?"

"Inevitability, I guess," he said, but that sounded too sweet-wine-ish, or Irish Crème mixed with soy milk, "Call it wishful thinking."

"Wishing what? Some other woman?"

He got up, walked into the kitchen next to his bedroom, ate an oatmeal cookie, like he ate every morning to cut down on bad cholesterol, thinking now how silly that was, as if he could put off death with oatmeal cookies.

"It would all be so great, death and resurrection, an eternity anywhere, even in Hell, anything but just turn off reality forever..."

"So you were dreaming about?"

"On the contrary, I was dreaming about when I had it great, the old days, les beaux années....before I met you...."

There's a fireplace in the bedroom, some fire-irons in a metal container next to the fireplace itself. She lightnings over to them and pulls out a long brass rod, antique-ish, very deadly-looking.

"You won't have to worry about your gold-plated past much longer," she hisses out.

"Very good!"

Then samurai-quick he grabs the rod out of her hand and tosses it on the floor, grabs her, a caress almost strong enough to break her ribs, and suddenly both of them soften, merge into each other, no words, no words needed.

WHAT DO YOU DO ON SUNDAYS?

What did we used to do on Sunday afternoons when I was a kid? We'd drive around in the Chicago suburbs and look at big-shot, beautiful houses. What do I do now a hundred years later? Drive around and look at big-shot, beautiful houses. Or maybe not just big-shot beautiful houses, but houses in old neighborhoods, the older the better. I'm looking for something I never had growing up – a house, a sense of neighborhood.

Did it make any sense? My mother's father, this skinny old streetcar conductor Irishman, had managed to buy a brick bungalow out in Cicero, west of Chicago. Great place. Dark red brick. Great attic. Great garden. Czech neighborhood. I remember my grandma talking over the back fence to her neighbors. In Czech. She was supposed to be Czech. Spoke Czech, said she was Czech.

But she wasn't Czech, she was Jewish.

But what did I know?

I went to Mass every morning. The Body and Blood of Christ. Of course now I know that Christ's Last Supper was a Passover dinner, but it wasn't until I went to my first Passover dinner after I'd converted to Judaism myself that I realized that the whole symbolism of the Body and Blood of Christ came from Passover symbolism, that the host that was Christ's body (transubstantiation, the real body of Christ, even though it just seemed to be an unleavened wafer) had symbolically begun as Passover matzas matzoth (plural of matzo/matzoh), the unleavened bread that the Jews ate in the desert – you know the whole "passing-over" into the Promised Land, out of Egypt thing. And the Passover wine became the symbol for Christ's blood. At age eight, nine, what did I know about such things? Nothing.

But came Easter, which is always around the time of Passover, and matzahs matzoth would appear on my grandmother's table with little glasses of oversweet but delicious dark purple kosher wine.

I always associated Matzahs matzoth and wine with Easter, and the association was there, right in the middle of the mass, but never spilled over into Catholic Easter services themselves. The mass was one big Passover supper all year long, but when my grandmother brought out her wine and matzahs matzoth I thought it must be something Czech. Czechs ate matzahs matzoth and drank wine at Easter.

When my grandmother would offer me a little glass of wine and some matzahs matzoth, my mother would object. My father had taken a Confirmation pledge to never touch a drop of alcohol, and he was so fanatic about it that he wouldn't even eat food that had any alcohol in it.

"No wine for the boy. Hugh will be furious if he finds out."

"What's a little wine going to hurt? It's good for you."

And she'd pour it for me anyhow. I hadn't made any pledges.

What a delicious combination, the dark, super-sweet purple kosher wine and the dark, crisp matzahs matzoth were.

Czechs were lucky, I thought, they had all the tasty stuff.

Then when Christmas came around, my grandmother would make stacks of potato pancakes. Potato pancakes and tea. She always drank a lot of tea.

What did I know about Chanukah? Nothing. Chanukah in the Jewish calendar always falls around Christmas. In fact that's why it's been turned from a super-minor feast in ancient times, to a super-big feast today. A little competition with Christmas now that Jews are part and parcel of a Christian world.

It was only a few years ago that I discovered the connection between my grandmother's Christmas potato pancakes and

Chanukah. Just to show share with you how retarded I am.

I converted to Judaism ten years ago, and had to go to attend conversion classes, learn Hebrew, the whole schmear. My professor was a guy named Bruce Wetzler, a cantor from New York. Wonderful guy. Great singer. Had been an enormous blimp of a guy man when he'd been younger but when I met him he was "normal"-sized, on a constant diet. Great singer. When he sang services it was classy, serious, timeless Judaism. And we became special friends. For years he invited me every year for Passover, when his daughters got married I was invited to the weddings, we'd go out to dinner, he and his wife, me and mine, say once a month. A Chinese restaurant called Gourmet Village ... and he'd order everything vegetarian item on the menu. Kosher from the word GO.

So here I am there I was dropping in on him a few years ago to bring him and his wife Miriam a Chanukah present and there's Miriam's in the kitchen cooking stacks of potato pancakes.

"How about a potato pancake?" she asks me, "I bet you've never had a potato pancake in your life."

"What are you talking about? My grandmother always used to make potato pancakes, stacks of them, just like you, right around Christmas."

Miriam poured me a cup of cocoa.

"My grandmother used to always have cocoa with the pancakes too."

Cantor Wetzler laughed. "Oh, brother, you were surrounded by the whole thing, but how could you have known?"

How could I have known?

Or Even my Uncle Jake. He was supposed to be James Mangan. His father was this bona fide Irishman, James Mangan Sr. I never heard him called anything but Jake.

He worked at the First National Bank in Chicago as a General Man. Which meant that he could fill in on any job in the bank. Some teller got sick, there he was, some Vice President was in Europe on vacation and here comes Jake to fill in for him.

And he ran his own business in the bank too. As wholesaler. anything you wanted, he could get it for you wholesale at a reduced price. You wanted a diamond ring, okay, out came the suitcase with samples in it. You wanted tires for your car, China for your cabinet, a fur coat for your wife, you name it, he had it.

Hardly your typical Irishman.

And there was a whole other world he was part of that I touched only peripherally once in a while.

He didn't just wholesale in the bank, but on Sundays (never on Saturdays, Sabbath, Note Bene!) he was always down in the Jewish wholesale district, and afterwards he'd be talking to my mother about Sol said this and Mort said that and Herb said that, it was a whole other life that I was never brought into except ....

There was one weird visit that I'll never forget no matter how long I live.

I must have been my eighth birthday. Jake took me down to Twelfth Street to this old toy store. We walked in, it was dark, super-crowded with toys. Everything you could imagine.

This old Jew came out of the back room.

"Hey, Jake!" Gave him a hug. "So you brought the boy."

And he practically started examining me like I was the patient and he was the doctor. Walked around and looked at me, me wondering the whole time what the hell was going on. "So you're eight. What kind of toys do you like? Are you into sports?"

"Not really. I like toy soldiers and guns, that kind of stuff."

"Ahhhhhh! Come back here."

He took me into the back of the store and took this big package down from a shelf, opened it up and pulled out a big khaki cannon.

"Let me show you how this works," the old guy said. "You put the powder in here in the top, put water in the cannon itself, then you press this little button, the powder falls into the water and that produces a gas. Then you press this other little button with a flint in it, it produces a spark, and BAM! It's the biggest sound you ever heard in your life. It's a little tricky, but it's safe. The powder is Calcium Carbide, when it comes into contact with water it produces Acetylene gas and that's what blows up. The cannon is cast iron. No problem. What do you think?"

I was overwhelmed. My own cannon. And all the fancy words, Calcium Carbide, Acetylene, made it sound a thousand times better cooler. "I love it."

"And you've gotta have some soldiers too," he said going over and getting two huge packages of lead soldiers and handing them to me, putting the cannon back in the box and handing it to Jake, still not just looking at me, but studying me like I was a lemur in a cage in a zoo or something. No one had ever been so interested in me before in my life. But it wasn't creepy, just filled with affection, tenderness. You could just feel that his hand wanted to come over and touch my hair. What was going on?

"So how much do I owe you?" Jake asked.

"Later, later," said the old guy waving Jake away Jake's gesture, half closing his eyes. It was just a normal "later," but something I translated as "forget it."

We still didn't leave and the old guy still kept studying me. I didn't want to leave, really. Felt some kind of strange, inexplicable bond between me and the old guy. But finally we did leave, the old guy gave Jake and me both hugs and we were out in the Chicago cold again. My birthday is February 12th. It was always the North Pole.

I think it was the only time Jake had ever taken me anyplace, just the two of us.

Why?

What was going on?

Who was the old guy?

Years later, when my grandmother was on her deathbed out in Arizona (living with Jake), my cousin Judy, one of Jake's daughters, was at her bedside, and here's what she told me later grandma told her a story. What follows is what Judy told me.

"Remember how Gram always said her family was Czech and that was it. All very vague. Well, she was dying and I was sitting there, no one else around, and she told me that when she was twelve her mother had died. She was deaf and the kids were sick and she'd gone out to get some food, and on the way back she didn't hear this train coming and she got hit by it and killed, and then her father married her mother's sister, which I thought sounded by weird, but she didn't get along with her aunt, her new mother, so she left home and got a job cleaning houses. That's how she made her living, cleaning houses. Then she met the Seidels and they took her in and treated her like a daughter, and she used to work in a bar serving drinks and when she got older she met this guy in the bar and they went out on a date, someplace way in the western part of Chicago, and he tried to rape her and she ran away and got to this street where there was this streetcar coming and she flagged it down and got on all hysterical and crying and the streetcar conductor was James Mangan, who became our grandfather. Only in order to get married in the Catholic Church, she had to 'convert,' or at least go through the motions, so she did ... and ... that's what she said. I've been thinking there was probably a lot more she didn't say."

Which really rang a bell for me.

She'd left her family when she was twelve.

When I was eight she must have been about fifty-five. If her father was twenty-five years older than her, that would make him about seventy. How old was the old guy in the toy store? About seventy? He couldn't have been my grandfather, could he? Could Jake have maintained contact with him over the years? Could the old man have asked him, "Come on, Jake, I just want to see the boy. He never has to know who I am ... just to see him..."

And Jake took me over to the toy store and..., It's an encounter I know I'll never forget.

Jake was a funny guy. Slicked back black hair when he was younger, always a little black moustache. Played saxophone when he was younger. Never went to church. And he never ate "normal" food.

On the way home from downtown Chicago every day he'd stop at Stop and Shop, this gigantic gourmet delicatessen, and buy kosher corned beef and potato salad, Jewish rye bread, Cole Slaw, kosher hot dogs. So when you went over to his house you always felt you were at Junior's restaurant in Brooklyn, the greatest little kosher restaurant in the world.

What did I know? To me it was all normal.

When my father's lawyer, Maurey Greiman, would come over to our house for Easter, my mother would serve ham, and Maurey would savor it with great relish, chewing it slowly and let the juices roll across his tongue, and say "This is the greatest salmon I've ever eaten."

Salmon? I thought it was ham.

My mother would laugh, and Natalie, Maurey's wife, would laugh. What was the big joke all about anyhow? What did I know about ham being one of the forbidden foods (along with shrimp) for Jews?

My mother knew, though. It was a sick game she was playing with Greiman.

She was in love with the guy, that was obvious. He and Natalie would always go to plays in downtown Chicago. Plays and concerts. And he'd talk about them, "Yeah, that Death of a Salesman was a real winner. I walked out feeling like I'd just been to a funeral. You pay your last payment on your house and then you die. Ha, ha, ha, ha ..."

"That's one thing we'll never have to worry about, paying a

last payment on a house," I almost said, but decided it was probably better that I shut up. Mainly, I just watched in those days, watched and listened.

Greiman liked to talk about Fritz Reiner conducting the Chicago symphony. "He's getting old, but he's still as precise as a surgeon, if you know what I mean."
My father would shake his head and smile. "I guess that's one thing I know."

My father had been a concert violinist before he'd met my mother. In fact had worked his way through pre-Med by playing in theater and cafe orchestras, when there still were theater and cafe orchestras. The library of books he had in a side room just off his office suggested just how literate he was – all of Dickens, Conan Doyle's The Lost World, William James' Psychology, a little Freud, Dumas.

After the Greimans would leave, my mother always talked about Maurey. "He's so cultured. All the plays and concerts they go to. It's so wonderful."

My father had turned into an old dead-head. I guess they had lots of sex, they were always getting rid of me, sending me to my grandmother's or to WMCA camp or to Bloom's Turkey Farm in Indiana, but apart from sex and going to eat at the Swedish Club, they didn't do much else.

My mother and Natalie Greiman used to go to the bazaars over at the South Shore Temple together with Natalie Greiman ... and it seemed that we were totally, always, surrounded by Jews. Was there anyone who wasn't Jewish?

Like I was sent to Catholic grammar school, but my best friend was Warren Halperin, who lived in the apartment building directly behind our apartment building at 756 East 82nd Street.

I think Warren's father was a lawyer too.

I was always over there or he was always over at my place.

And across the street was Weiner, the tailor, my dentist was

Dr. Lerner, just catty corner from my father's office.

My father had had his first office on 79th street and he'd become friends with a Dr. Morris, a dentist, and w When I was about twelve we moved over to 8047 S. Maryland, just across the street from the Morrises.

Dr. Morris's wife was Fanny, kind of soft and round, with long dyed henna hair.

I was told to call her "aunt." Aunt Fanny.Aunt Fanny and Dr. Morris.

My parents were so close with the Morrises that one time we even went down to Miami with them. 8047 S. Maryland was right across the street from the Am Echod Synagogue and that's where the Cub Scouts and Boy Scouts had their meetings. So I was enrolled in the Cub Scouts and off to the synagogue I went every week to the Cub Scouts, fascinated by the old Jews I'd see there wearing their shawls and little skull caps, always saying hello, "Howya doin'?," serious to the point of solemn, but always cordial.

And then there were all the Jews downtown.

I never, never, ever bought a readymade suit. Everything was tailor-made. The same was true of my father's clothes. The tailor was a Jew down on Van Buren Street.

"Mrs. Fox, how are youuu?"

Very special treatment – my mother all dolled up with her mink stole and stockings and ankle strap alligator shoes, right off the big screen, she was Bette Davis, Joan Crawford, Lana Turner.

I remember one tailor, a Mr. Siegel, who invited us to his place in Ludington, Michigan. A house on the lake. A Victorian with an arbor filled with roses. We ate knishes and bagels and fresh pears and peaches.

Just like home.

Did everyone go and visit their tailor's summer home on Lake Michigan? Or wasn't my mother always being treated like a Jew by Jews?

There was something very special about the way Maurey Greiman treated my grandmother. Mrs. Mangan this, Mrs. Mangan that.

He knew, didn't he?

One time, when I was over at the Greiman's place in South Shore alone, Maurey walked with me along the street car line just for fun. I told him "You know, the Jews are a very special people, the Chosen People in a way, the people that God chose to make Himself known to." I remember him reaching over and giving me a little hug. But that's the way I felt, the way I had been trained.

All the early Christians had been Jews. The biggest part of the Bible was the Old Testament. Christ was a Jew. And I had always been surrounded by Jews. Did everyone else know about my mother and grandmother? Was I the only one who hadn't been told?

I remember little things like my father talking to my grandmother in the corner of the living room of our apartment on Maryland Avenue. Something about language. He knew German, had studied German, he had a German mother. And my grandmother knew Czech. Only what were they comparing, German and Czech? Now, after studying German and Yiddish myself, of course, I know that Yiddish is a kind of South German dialect, and that my father and grandmother must have been comparing German and Yiddish, words like "bad," shlekht (Yiddish) and "to be," schlecht (German), zayn (Yiddish) and zu sein (German), "back" as in "to return," tsurik (Yiddish) and zuruck (German).

But I wasn't supposed to know that my grandmother spoke Yiddish, was I?

My uncle Jake would use Yiddish expressions, good guys would be mentshes, congratulations would be mazel tov, but every time he'd drop a little Yiddish my mother would give him a dirty look. The secret had to be kept at all costs.

We weren't Jewish. We were Catholic.

Although ... I remember one Christmas, my father insisted that my grandmother come to Mass with us. I remember watching her enter St. Francis de Paulo church looking at the big, beamed, painted ceiling. The images of Christ's death in the stained glass windows – the fourteen Passions/Stations of the Cross – and the huge crucifix hanging from the ceiling directly above a magnificent marble altar in front.

All of which immensely impressed her. Impressed her and confused and interested her. She obviously wasn't in familiar territory. I remember her saying, her face was saying "What's all this all about anyhow?"

We sat down and somehow, in the course of the Mass itself, instead of the usual normal collection of monies from the congregation and one special Christmas collection, the usher came around three times, and the third time Gram laughed and took out her false teeth.

"If he comes around once more I'm going to give him my teeth," she said. "They're really hard up (Would she use this term? Did she?) around here, aren't they?"

There were messages being piped my way full time.

When we'd go grocery shopping my grandmother, widowed as she was, living on my streetcar conductor grandfather's pension, baby-sitting for twenty-five cents an hour, she would immediately go directly to the Last Chance-Almost Garbage racks. She bought meat that was a little blackish, still edible, but you'd better cook it fast or it wouldn't be. And corn meal muffins that were a little on the hard side – she'd serve them with lots of butter and jelly and tea and you wouldn't even notice. Hard bread. Bananas you had to cut the bruises out of. Peaches that you had to carefully carve to remove the inedible parts.

But when it came time to eat, everything was always delicious.

The message – you turn evil into good.

And never let anything get you your spirits permanently down.

There was one couple she used to baby-sit for. The Bernsteins. They always gave her a nice tip and drove her home instead of letting her walk that one dark block back to her place alone. Especially in the winter.

And She always made a point of saying they were Jewish.

Always a sense of camaraderie, tribalness the tribe.

One night, they, the Bernsteins, didn't drive her home. Probably hot to trot or just too tired. It was the middle of winter and she my grandmother walked home, as usual down the alley, the way I always used to do, figuring it's safer the darker and more isolated it is, like squirrels disappearing into thickets or bats under roof tiles in Quito. Only she fell down on the ice. Fell down and broke her hip, and still managed to drag herself home, up the how many flights of stairs, and knocked on our apartment door, which was right next to hers.

"Ma, are you crazy?!? What's wrong with those people, damn them anyhow!" my mother screaming at her, waking up half the apartment house apartment building.

"It's not their fault," my grandmother said. "I fell down. I ought to get some flat-soled shoes and boots for the winter."

My father rushed her to the hospital and he put her back together again. He'd do anything, broken bones, any surgery imaginable (except the brain).

She recovered fine, within a couple of months she wasn't even limping any more, back baby-sitting with the Bersteins again. And they'd always drive her home even in the middle of summer.

Sometimes I'd knock on her door, dusk, mid-winter, everything frozen outside, the sun down by five-thirty, and she'd call out "Hey, come on in."

I'd go in and there she would be in the living room. Second

floor, no lights on, just sitting there looking out on the street, Dr. Lerner's office catty-corner from my father's office, an apartment house just across the street, a National Tea grocery store on the first floor next to a Chinese restaurant and Weiner's tailor shop. The street always busy. Stoplight. A streetcar stop just outside my grandma's window. Always 'the blues' and my dead grandfather. Like a formula, prayer, miserere nobis, have mercy on us, baruch atta Adonai, God is great......

"So how you doin', Gram?"

"I've got the blues."

"About what?"

"Everything. Just thinking about your dead grandfather, it'll be seven years since his death. September 21st."

As glum as anyone could get. Kaddish, Kaddish, Kaddish. Jews who you haven't seen for months will appear at the synagogue on a Friday night, and then the Rabbi reads out the names of the people whose death-anniversaries occur that week. Ah, Max Dorn, there he is, it's the anniversary (jahrzeit) of his father's death this week.

Not that the Jews pray for the souls of the dead like the Catholics, edging them into Heaven if they aren't already there.

It's just remembering, always remembering, part of a vast sea of The Past. All the Kaddish prayer does, really, is praise God. Any idea of an afterlife in Judaism (sheol) completely vague and tenuous.

But I was there, wasn't I, and that was enough to perk her up. That was the other side of the coin of Jewish thinking about the afternoon. We are all like candles that burn down and are gone forever, but part of us lives on in our children and grandchildren and great grandchildren, ad infinitum.

I was picking up all sorts of things, wasn't I? To see life as essentially tragic, finite, no big dreams of wonderous afterlives, concentrate on the here and now because that's all you have.

Concentrate on your children and grandchildren because they are what carry your genetic you into the future. And at the same time don't really let anything get you down, you're tough, you're hard, you're durable....and little quips and silly jokes are what get you through Time, as God, up there in the heavens (and in your innermost heart) keeps the world rolling.

On one hand I had the official Catholic ideas about afterlives, heavens and hells and purgatories, being pumped into me, but more intimately, on an everyday level, there was my grandmother's example of endurance....always a bit in a minor key, always with a touch of humor and cynicism, but always affirmative, tough, enduring....

I was being turned into a Jew without the slightest hint about the process.

I was only two when my grandfather died. But I still remember him. Weird. He used to always buy me all kinds of tweed caps and I remember him bending over and putting this tweed cap on my head and telling me "Always wear a nice tweed cap, me boy, there's nothing like a nice tweed cap." And here I am at 68, and guess what, I wear full-time? A a nice tweed cap. I've got a whole collection of them nice tweed caps in the downstairs closet by the front door. A whole shelf full of them.

My grandfather didn't have any education beyond high school (if he had that), but he still managed to buy a brick bungalow and raise a family. My father was an M.D. and we always lived in apartments. And hated it.

Like our apartment right next to my grandmother's place on 756 East 82nd Street in Chicago. Eighty second and Cottage Grove Avenue. Cottage Grove, my ass. No cottages, no groves.

But Larsen's bakery was right downstairs of the apartment. Both Mr. and Mrs. Larson were from Sweden. Which was nice, having a basement bakery right downstairs. I remember fresh the breads dusted with flour, fresh, fresh, fresh, you'd break open the crust and you'd be eating clouds.

Right next to Larsen's was a bar that was full-time noise. Especially in the summers. No air-conditioning. And you know Chicago, off the lake. Way up into the nineties full time in the summers. You had to leave the windows open. The streetcar ran all night and you slept with a fan blowing on you. There'd always be fights downstairs in the bar that would erupt out onto the street. I remember Mrs. Graziano one time getting stabbed, and the next thing you knew they were banging on the door of our apartment.

"Hey, Doctor Fox, Mrs. Graziano's just gotten stabbed."

Of course he got up. He had h His office was on the corner, right next to the apartment.

I didn't have to get up. I was already there, when he opened the door me standing right next to him. And there was He opened the door with me right beside him and Mrs. Graziano with a guy on each side holding of her up, blood gushing out of her chest, these huge tits, black hair (dyed), stiletto thin skyscraper heels. A real piece of woman.

"Come to my office," my father said. I followed, and in they went, me following right close behind. Washed his hands, put on a white gown and rubber gloves. Got her up on the operating table and he gave her some either, went right in, no limit to his daring, opened up the chest, found the limits of the wound, started sewing, putting her back together.

Amazing guy. Great doctor.

Like the time when I was out in one of the empty lots on the same block and I fell down on some broken milk bottles and cut my left leg, all the way down to the bone. Arteries severed. Tendons. Walked Made it three-quarters of a block, supported by two pals of mine, and he my father put me up on the table and did the whole job right there where Mrs Graziano was laying. I'm still walking on it, right?

He would have been great in an emergency room.

Or like the time I came home from my grandmother's place in Cicero. My grandfather was already dead, but she was managing to hang on to the house anyhow. I'd been there for a couple of months. They used to farm me out to her for the summer. And I'd been swimming in the neighborhood pool.

I got into my father's black Chevy (that was before he moved up to big black Buicks) and he gave me a long, medical look.

"You look red. Too red. It's not sunburn," he said, reaching over and touching my forehead, put your chin down on your chest.

"Chin on my...?"

"Try to put your chin on your chest."

I tried but couldn't do it.

"My God, it's polio," he said. No hesitation, or fumbling around, "Michael Reese-Sarah Lawrence hospital. That's where you're going. Let me go tell your mother. Wait here."

And up the back stairs of our apartment house building he went. He was pudgy but fast . A grey silk suit on wearing a gray silk suit. Tie. It was hard to imagine him taking a bath or having sex or ever taking his tie off without a tie. Tie and Doctor. Loved to be called Doctor. Doctor Fox this, Doctor Fox that. He was like a horse born to be a racer. You couldn't imagine him doing anything else. Although ... there was another him that was totally dead now, the violinist-him, the opera-lover him, the artiste, that he'd totally suppressed when my mother had pushed him into toward Medicine.

He was back down to the car in about five minutes with my mother, as always dressed to the hilt. Even in the midst of a Chicago summer heat-wave. Beige stockings and white high heels with ankle straps, always ankle-straps, if they didn't have ankle straps they weren't shoes, a white linen dress with all sorts of flounces, her hair all frilled and curled and marcelled, wearing enough makeup to turn a horse into a zebra. Carrying a little black leather bag in one hand, a white purse over her shoulder. Sun glasses on. You always wore sunglasses during the day in order to avoid the slightest possibility of squinting and creasing up the skin around your eyes. Wrinkles were anathema. At night when she went to bed she'd be so greased up that she'd look like a sliced bagel smeared with cream cheese.

"I told Ma not to take him to that public swimming pool!" she was squealing as she came down the wooden porch stairs.

What was Queen Helen coming down a flight of crumby old wooden back-porch stairs for anyhow? They should have been marble stairs with alabaster railings leading down to the coach-house where her minions would have been standing at attention with the door to the Rolls Royce open and waiting for her highness.

All this faulty economics crap that my father would forever be mouthing about "I never buy anything unless I can pay cash for it." If the pharaohs, kings, popes and tycoons of the past had subscribed to that kind of nonsense the great pyramids, Versailles, St. Peters, Westminster Abbey and the Empire State Building would never have been built.

"I suppose you had to go swimming, you couldn't listen to your mother," she started in on me as my father opened the door for her and she started to get in. Then she stopped, addressed me very snippily, "Get in the back, you'll be more comfortable," I got out and she assumed her proper place in the front seat.

She reached back and touched me on the forehead.

"He's burning up."

"They're doing some research down at Michael Reese," my father said. "There's this new serum treatment they're working on." He pulled out of the parking lot behind Gorman's grocery and Joe's barber shop, down the alley past the Catalpa trees in Warren Halperin's backyard that I'd climb in and come home smelling of humus and old inner tubes because that's what the leaves smelled like.

"What if it goes into his lungs?" My mother started in as my father drove down 82nd Street to Cottage Grove and then turned north.

"No 'what if's' at this point," he said. "We'll just do what we have to do. He may die. Lots of kids do. And he's our only one; don't know what we would do without him."

My mother had "lost" one child when she was putting my father through medical school. She was working as a secretary. Well, not exactly "lost." If she'd gotten pregnant and had had to quit working, my father wasn't going to finish medical school. Never a thought about student loans, I guess, in those days. So anything but him not finishing medical school. She went down to work at Diamond T the day after she found out she was pregnant, and started lifting all the heaviest boxes she could find. Miscarried. And then, when he'd finished medical school she had me, then a tubal pregnancy and my father operated and tied off both her fallopian tubes. So that was it. No more possibilities for any more kids. She was always the pain and discomfort it caused her. Every month during ovulation when an egg would drop and die.

"We can always adopt, there's all kinds of kids around," she said, "although I don't want any Chinese or Mexicans or."

"Don't worry about it, Helen, we're doing all we can...."

And she stopped. Rolled down the windows.

"This heat. It's worse than Florida."

"Nothing's worse than Florida," I said beginning to kind of lose it by this time, "reality" out there beyond me getting vaguer and vaguer as I floated further and further into the self-enclosed world of high fever.

We hadn't gone down to Florida this summer yet but lots of summers we did. Miami, always some big hotel right on the beach. Summer rates. Because nobody wanted to be there. It was like spending a week in a steam bath. Although I always kind of liked it because, when you went swimming, the ocean was almost as hot as the air. None of that painful shock of jumping into cold water like jumping into Lake Michigan and you'd feel like someone was sticking an icicle up your ass.

"Just count your blessings, my dear," my mother said, turning around and touching me. Then reporting to my father, "He's as hot as a burning log." And asking me "Can you move your legs?"

I moved them.

"I guess so."

"I'd hate to see him spend the rest of his life in an iron lung," she said to my father.

"Not to mention the expense."

I began to entirely lose it. All it was heat, heat and more heat, cars, streetcars, the "L" overhead. We crossed 63rd Street, then 55th and the University of Chicago where my father had gone to pre-Med, before he enlisted for World War I and had a bout of typhoid fever that landed him in a hospital in France for most of the war, which ultimately brought him back to Chicago, where he forgot the idea of medicine altogether, took a job in the First National Bank as a teller, where he met my mother's brother, James … Uncle Jake.

We passed the Rockefeller Chapel where years later I'd go to study Physics when I was in pre-Med (at Loyola) myself, forced into it by my parents. An M.D. or else. That's all life was about, M.D.'s, although an M.D. didn't buy you a house, did it?

"The damned Larsons, why start baking at five A.M., all the noise, and the smells....especially in the summer.....how are you supposed to sleep through the smells of baking bread, rolls, coffee cakes....." Another one of my mother's constant refrains.

Down past Passed the Museum of Science and Industry, another one of my favorite places, a relic from a nineteenth century world's fair (why had they ever torn anything down from the glorious neo-classical past?), and along Lake Michigan, gloriously cool for a moment. Gulls and waves. Down the Outer Drive. Who planned these wonders? Who were the giants behind the plans of our glorious cities?

The next thing I remember was being in the hospital in a white gown tied in back. I was still a human furnace, and I couldn't walk and they were putting me up on an operating table and there was this doctor standing there with an enormous hypodermic syringe in his hand. My father was there too. And the other doctor told him, "You realize, Doctor Fox, that we've only done experiments on monkeys so far. No humans. There is a possibility that the injection could kill the boy."

"I understand," my father said fatalistically. "But I'd rather he was dead than crippled."

And that was it. In went the syringe. Right into my spinal column, prying it apart, the most excruciating pain I'd ever felt. Crucifixion couldn't have been any worse. The pain was at the very core and center of my whole being. It was like someone taking a sledgehammer and banging me at the base of my spine. Then it was over.

"Okay, let's see what happens." Do you want to attribute this quote to anyone?

Technically I'd always been a Jew. In Judaism the Jewish line goes through the female and my grandmother being a Jew, my mother was technically a Jew and so was I. But eventually, in my late forties, having reached total agnosticism, and having discovered the truth about my Jewish family past, I went over to the local synagogue in East Lansing, took a course in Judaism, went through a mainly symbolic circumcision (a couple of drops of blood), went through a Bar Mitzvah, and haven't missed a Friday night surface for some thirty years, feel very much part of the local community, almost like being in shetlel/village somewhere in Lithuanian back in the eighteenth century. My wife's father was

Jewish, she "converted," her brother did the same, as did his wife and my ex-wife, my two younger daughters and son converted....I brought a whole boat load of family in with me. No negatives, just a beautiful sense of belonging to a world-view that says sanity, peace, brother-love...enjoy...

MIRIAM MEETS FATHER PEGUY

She loved Paris, period. Wasn't much that she didn't love.

Loved to simply walk along the Seine, practically anywhere, the trees, the lovers, l'histoire, especially now that she'd been (rather painfully) immersing herself in French history, literature, reinforcing what she already knew about Satie and Baudelaire, Monet, Renoir, Apollinaire....dragging herself through the Louvre over and over again during the afternoons before she picked up les enfants at school, Adam more confused than she was at their sudden immersion in French culture after ten years of pure Hebrew-Israeli-Jewish everything, although in a way Michael was already at home, given his long-term penchant for everything Francaise.

"How long are we going to stay here?" Adam had asked the night before as she bent down to kiss him as he lie there in his bed, sleepy as a drunken dormouse, "I miss the beach..."

"France has beaches too. Not too far...if we can just save a little money. If I could write a book about my leaving Israel and coming to Paris...
someone over at Am Echod..."

Which gave her the giggles. And made her feel ashamed.

Not that she'd forgotten Mort, engulfed as he was in tragedy, never able to undo that final image on the stretcher, half his head gone, all drenched in his own blood, like some sort of (non-Kosher style) slaughtered ox...

But it was true, it seemed a trifle remote now...all of it...the whole ancient war of Israel for its own territory, Babylonians, Philistines, Egyptians, Palestinians...whoever, whoever, whoever, especially when...

La pluie est fraiche,
le ventre est bon...

The rain is fresh,
the wind is good.

Loved Artaud. Struggled through him with her Hebrew-French dictionary....

It was so nice to be able to speak Hebrew with Rabbi Frankel over at Am Echod, even if it was work, work, work, major work for him. Good for him.

Sometimes in unguarded, off moments an image coming into her mind of them together, completely naked, in the midst of high passion.

Shame, shame....

Although how could he stand that groundhog wife of his with her intolerable hats and shoes and bowed-legs and gold glasses and vanity, vanity, vanity?

And there was always a touch of, what would you call it, "flirtation," in the air:

Il dit non avec la tete
mais il dit oui avec le coeur...

He says no with his head
but he says yes with his heart...

Forget it, forget it!

Walking down the left bank toward Notre Dame now, thinking of Hemingway and Fitzgerald and Henry Miller...the avant-garde American literary gang here in the twenties, before World War II...

Too much reading, she was becoming such a nerd.

But loving the trees along the Seine, especially now that Fall was arriving, the summer heat was gone, it was almost chill, and most of the tourists had left.

Why so attracted to Notre Dame?

It was as if her subconscious had taken over her legs and she was walking there not against her will, but without any will at all, dreamlike, dans un reve.

Thinking all sorts of...what would you call them, "sacriligious" thoughts?

Judaism didn't give any ultimate answers, did it, God up there in the sky somewhere, pulling up and pulling down the sun and moon, keeping the stars in place, blessing us with life...and death...

Kaddish again, per omnia saecula saeculorum, for all time-eternity, haolam. She should have never bought the missal she'd bought two weeks ago...the prayers for the dead full of Hollywoodish heavens, clouds and angels and...that other book she'd gotten on Catholicism..The Beatific Vision, pushed to the peak of all possible pleasure, forever and forever, Amen.

Not like Kaddish, where all you did was praise God, praise God, praise God.

A street vendor up ahead. Wraps. A little chicken wrap wouldn't hurt her.

Everything from the street-vendors in Paris always so good.

"Treat yourself a little,," her voices inside her whispering. She was doing okay teaching at the Am Echod Hebrew school, although sometimes she thought that Rabbi Frankel was overpaying her, something under-the-table-ish about it all, because she was a survivor from Israel, a widow whose husband had been practically pulverized by The Enemy, because she was her...

A big mirror in the window of an antique store, something very Italianate, nineteenth centuryish, nicely carved wooden scrolls, obviously the mirror itself new, stopped and looked at herself in it...

The darkish perfect skin, very black eyes and black (dyed) hair, the little hat-cap, ankles and legs so amazingly slim, remembering her buba even when she was in her forties, how her ankles had swollen up and stayed that way, probably the tight stockings she always wore, tight bands around the tops cutting off circulation, not like pouring yourself into liquid nylon pantyhose....

Rabbi Frankel back again, looking at her, as if he were embarrassed somewhere deep inside himself, embarrassed for being, for...being in love with her?

Not that she could blame him, thinking about his wife again, Sarah's, stubby little fatsy-watsy legs. Not to mention her face, always looking like she'd just eaten a hot pepper.

And how did she feel about him?

"Horney" wasn't the word. Not "physical," really but missing another body against hers, missing naked contact, penetration, climaxing, then the collapse back on the bed, someone in her arms and her in someone's arms, like two naked babies sleeping together, beyond sex altogether....thinking about "heaven" again....what did they call it, extreme unction? No that was something else...

Going over to the street vendor, who looked very "Arabish," not Palestinian but further northern, maybe into Jordan or Afghanistan. Tempted to try a little Arabic on him, mais non, non, non.....

"A chicken wrap, si vous plait...."

Smiling, very gracious.

Tres cher, but so what, everything in Paris was expensive, especially around here, "downtown." Thrifty, always thrifty, in spite of being "loaded" (in the bank/stocks/investments, like "theory"), happy to have found such a nice (albeit tiny) place in a working class neighborhood. One bedroom, so let the kids sleep in it, she didn't mind the sleeper-sofa, and the traffic noise outside that she'd thought would have bothered her, actually seemed to soothe her to sleep...although she missed the sound of the sea that she'd loved so much in Tel Aviv. Feeling sometimes guilty about just how much she had in the bank, the interest that she (mainly) lived on, even letting a little bit flow back into the capital itself.

Sea, sea, sea....why such a fascination with the sea?

In the beginning...the sea in the beginning...as if we were all just sea-things that had made their way by chance to land.

Thinking about the Gospel of, what was it, John: In the beginning was the Word, and the Word was God, and the Word was with God....

Why was she reading the gospels at all?

Almost as if it were a "sin." Was she picking up the Catholic-Christian sense of "sin" too? Christ was the "Word" spoken by God the Father. Only if the Messiah was Jesus of Nazareth, why wasn't the world inflated with, what could you call it, "messiah-ness?" saved, jubilant, rejoicing, instead of toujours, toujours triste/forever, forever sad...? If there were any God up there why didn't He step out on a cloud or something and bang His scepter on the earth and stamp out violence, appear in all His glory and stop the crap...

Melech Haolam! / King of the Universe! Why would any king allow his universe to degenerate into such a mess?

Bit into the wrap. Ahhhhhhh...better than sex. Blue cheeseish, roquetfortish, with a touch of humus, which made the vendor an Arab, n'est pas?

Reminding her of the kibe sandwiches/wraps her mother used to buy her on the streets of Tel Aviv and Jerusalem when she was a kid, before all this crap had begun.

Finding a bench next to the river and sitting down.

Something to drink?

No....don't spoil it with anything else...chew it slowly, savor it, and then later a coke...a beer...

Paris so romantic...all the fancy stores and apartment buildings, the river itself so carefully tended and contained in stone channels...so romantic, if you didn't think about kings and revolutions and guillotines and riots and World War II and Buchenwald.....

Shushhing herself.

"Quiet! Quiet! Calm!"

Reading Suzuki's Zen Mind, Beginner's Mind right now, kind of Talmudish-Kaballistic, calm, calm, calm, let the negative flow through you to the Great Sea of Nothingness...as if all we were was flowers, a brief blooming and then shalom, peace, peace, peace...

Enjoying the leaves on the maple tree over her, enjoying the bright white, clouded-over sky, almost crisp already, early September, the High Holidays coming up, which she'd have to go to, wouldn't she, being part of the faculty at the Am Echod Hebrew School and all, but which she had begun to hate, the endlessness of it all, all the self-recrimination, asking God for forgiveness...

For what?

She felt almost saintly, sinless...alone, sexless, chaste, pure, a good mother, a good teacher, a good friend....

Lo, lo, lo, lo.....Thou halt Not!

Shalt not what?

Adultery, theft, murder...

Maybe Commandment number one: I AM THE LORD THY GOD, THOU SHALT NOT HAVE STRANGE GODS BEFORE THEE...

Right out of the Douay version of the bible that she'd bought.

Wasn't Jesus a "strange" god.

Echod, echod, echod. One.....no trinities.....but sometimes, when she was walking along she could almost feel the Holy Spirit/Espiritu Sancto fluttering around her shoulders like a chiffon

122

ghost....Heilige Gaste...where had she read about the Anglo-Saxon (or was it German?) Heilige Gaste, Holy Ghost.....which they'd modified to Holy Spirit...

No ghosts, just spirits.

Okay, warm me , Holy Spirit, cuddle around my shoulders like a warm, wool shawl.

Making a big effort to get out of her head and speculations and simply enjoy the sandwich that she carefully held so it wouldn't drip on her brown knit blouse, not looking forward to the real cold, having to get her coats out of the closet, coats and boots...and worry about the boys getting cold...which they always did, no matter what she did.

Missing the heat of Tel Aviv, the whole Israeli coast.

Loving Lebanon. Past tense now...loving the sound of Arabic next to Hebrew. Past tense. Loving the intensity of the Arabs themselves. Past tense. Arab food...no, that didn't have to be past tense.

Finishing up the wrap, down to its last fragment of tomato, the last drop of its spicy, minaret-ish juice....

Loving the Alhambra in Sevilla, the way the Jews practically "ran" Arab Spain. Remembered her Kaballistic grandfather telling her how he had lived in Safed, the home of the Kaballah, for years....and loved his Arab neighbors.

If the Israelis had just never started "colonizing" into the middle of what was de facto "Arab territory"...maybe no conflicts would ever have arisen...

Licking her fingers, taking a handkerchief out of her brown leather purse and wiping her fingers with it. Mrs. (Professor) Perfect. The vendor still standing not far away, doing a good business. Waving at him, a little Arabic, "Salaam!" Shalom....and he waved smiling, "Salaam!"

Down to the bridge over to Cité and Notre Dame.

Time for a little art meditation, history-of-cathedrals

meditation....

Be honest with yourself, call it what it is, a love-affair with Jesus.

The voices inside her almost (but still not quite!) real voices.

When she'd told the Rabbi about the "voices" inside her talking, usually contradicting what she was saying, trying to think, he told it was "normal, normal, normal...we all self-dialogue with ourselves...there are all kinds of different fragmented selves inside us, each of them trying to take over."

But she'd gone to a psychiatrist who had wanted to put her on pills.

"We don't psychoanalyze much anymore. It's all biochemical now. Pills do it all."

Which she didn't want to get involved with. Took some St. John's Wort for a while, but that seemed to make her worse, was getting just as distrustful of herbs as prescription drugs.

Like the time she'd taken Kava Kava to help her sleep and had turned into a sexed-up madwoman and had actually 'done it' to herself, which she'd never done before.

Two days of Kava Kava, practically climbing roofs. The fiddler on the roof alright....David and Bathsheba....Salome dropping her last veil....

Approaching the front of Notre Dame now, the magnificent facade that invariably inspired awe in her.

"I'm back!" she said to the facade, the towers.

The Virgin Mary with the infant Jesus on her lap, the bible open in his hand, making him a child-scholar, and the Virgin Mary herself carrying a scepter in her hand, crowned with a beautiful crown, the Queen and her child, no king around except the infant Christ, King Of The Universe...Melech haolam.....haolam....olam ....the universe and eternity......

Taking a notebook out of her purse and starting to draw.

The beatifically calm face of the Virgin. Buddhistic. The

Buddha of Kamakura, beyond flesh, in a state of absolute calm, what a strange word to come into her head, "redemptive" ....redemptive calm....not that she knew anything about "redemption." Except during the high holidays...the rest of the year you were what you were what you were...

The child Jesus.

God becoming man....but really becoming man, finding out what becoming a man was really about.

Again perfect Buddhistic calm.

His right hand up blessing the world...

Was just beginning to sketch in the "frame" surrounding the virgin and child, the Corinthian columns and then the "city" on an arch over their head, the City of God speaking to the City of Man...

When a tall, thin priest came walking along.

Old, old, old.

Wondering, do priests ever, ever retire....? Or was it like the pope -- 'til Death us do Part!

"Tres joli! /Very beautiful!"

"Merci!/ Thanks!"

"Do I detect a bit of a foreign accent in that 'merci'?' You're from...? "

"Israel. Tel Aviv."

"Don't tell me. You know about Jews for Jesus?"

"Not really. I'm...how should I put it...'my own person.' Not much of a joiner. More rebel than anything else. I do a lot of reading. I've been doing a lot more the last few months. The New Testament.St. Paul, all kinds of books about Catholicism. It seems the second hand bookstores are filled with them. My apartment is starting to turn into a mini-library...."

"Well...I don't 'pressure' people, but if you're ever interested in, how shall I put it, 'converting,' it's a word that sounds so abrasive, like sandpaper, if you're ever interested in 'sandpapering' your soul..," laughing now, ancient gold glasses that looked like they came out of some flea market somewhere, antique, long hair falling over his forehead, what was he, ninety or something, but very 'engaging,' nothing fake about him, coming on as someone genuine, nothing in it for him, and beside the joviality a deep Buddhistic, yes, that was the word, Buddhistic calm..., "my name is Father Peguy...and, yes, I'm a distant cousin of the writer, do you know Peguy?"

"Not really, I've only been here a little more than a year."

"Mais vous-parlez tres bien....il semble que vous-etes ici plus que vente anneés.../ But you speak very well. It seems that you are here more than twenty years."

Inventing, of course. Twenty. Why not make it forty? Why not have me being born in the Bois du Bologne on the coldest day in Parisian history, turn me into a legend?

"Anyhow, I live here at Notre Dame. In fact I even have a card," going into his pants pocket, under his black gown, pulling out a card and handing it to her, "I even have an e-mail....Jesus, the computer nerd," laughing again, then repentant, "I take that back...no joking about redeemers, n'est pas?/isn't that true?"

" C'est vrai, oui/very true, yes...that would be like a Rabbi joking about Moses and the ten commandments ..."

Getting very solemn for a moment.

"We're kind of all the same eggs in the same basket anyhow..."

"Only different kinds of birds," she couldn't help but laughing, her old grandmother's genes in her, refusing to take anything, anything, anything serious, even on her deathbed, her last words, "So long, so long, just watch out for those latkes..."

Latkes, potato pancakes...

Chanukah.

Wondering, for a quick lightning bolt of a moment, what the connection was between the winter solstice, Christmas (Christ as reborn sun-god?) and Chanukah...and potato pancakes.

"Well...listen...remember...Father Peguy...if you have any questions, anything at all, you know where I am. E-Mail, whatever, I love e-mail, don't you? I used to know a Cecilia Guilarte in Toloso, Spain. She'd written a book on Santa Teresa and had written to me because she'd come across my name in her researches, and then I lost contact with her, looked her up on the internet the other day, not expecting to find her, but there she was, dead, unfortunately, but very much alive on the internet..."

"I don't have a computer myself, but there is one over at the synagogue that I use..."

"Synagogue?"

"Enghein."

"Oh, yes, I've been there. I love Enghein, Le Lac des Cygnes, even if it is connected to the casino. I'm very, how, shall I put it, trans-cultural...," taking her hand, smiling, a quick shake, "Shalom, shalom, shalom...or as we put it, at least 'used' to put it before Vatican II, Pax Vobiscum...," let her hand loose and was about to go, but had to put in a few last words, amusing her, seeing him as Father, P.S., P.S., P.S., "I liked Latin, the connection with Rome...the time of Christ's crucifixion...just that little linguistic link to the past..."

"What about French?" she laughed, "It's Latin too..."

"Not anymore," he laughed and was out the door with a wave, as she continued to draw the Virgin and Christ child, thinking, oddly enough, surprised at how insanely her mind worked, about how the whole time she was growing up in Tel Aviv, during services she'd had to sit with the other women in a special place at the back of the synagogue, and wear a 'veil,' not exactly a veil...but the connection with the Moslems was there, everything male-centered...except with the Catholics suddenly you went back to the Magna Mater religions of the ancient Mediterranean, didn't you, all the cathedrals in France, almost all of them, huge monuments to the Virgin, Notre Dame of This,

Notre Dame of That...the Great Mother behind everything...as if the whole universe were somehow created not by, but out of her..motherplasm...and the male somehow subordinated to her.....even the Christ child, the son of God...

GENEOLOGY

Old, once white, ten percent dissolved wood farmhouse on the edge of an unpaved road, up, up, they always had to be up, porch and out-buildings in back, a shabby dismantling barn, perfect albeit antique silo.

"So this is it," said Jerry, the country-know-it-all guide, "I don't wanna try to drive away...you never know...look around if you want, half an hour and then we can go back into town, we've got another hour and twenty minutes before sundown, and dusk lingers out here..."

The former farm fields, stubble remnants of old corn, apple trees with half-mature apples on them. No broken windows, the roof still kind of shambley but intact.

"You can just leave, I'm staying overnight."

"Listen," hesitating, weak and wobbly for a moment, and then bayonetish stuff, "I just can't let you out here like this. It's dangerous, there's animals, like black bears, coyotes....you never know...I've seen porcupines."

Pat reaches into his pocket. A hundred dollar bill. Hands it to the driver.

"Even worse...bribes...I don't say this place belongs to anyone any more, but..," but the driver still takes it, acts like he doesn't want to, "the first time in thirty years I've seen a hundred dollar bill. So what are you gonna do tonight, what about food? You know..."

"I've got some stuff in my pockets."

"Well..." And he backs away slowly, reluctantly, goes to his ancient, constantly-being-fixed Ford, stops with a certain medieval solemnity. "So when do I pick you up?"

Sam takes out his cell-phone, points to it.

"A bientot!"

"Whatever! I suppose I'm supposed to be impressed, but I'm more than im...I trust all will go well. You'll end up with the birds in the old corn fields looking for one last kernel. Although I think even that's stopped fifty years ago."

"Of uncommon sense."

One last sigh that says impatience, he's a real patient and needs HELP, HELP,

HELP...and he's off and gone, Sam wondering if he even put on his safety belt.

"Ah, well..."

Up to the front door. Locked. Curtains still on the windows, but he can see wooden columns inside, always loved/loves wooden columns in entrance ways, between rooms, down the sagging wood steps amazingly well-preserved, always loving old/ancient concrete block houses out in the middle of nowhere like here, the blocks as unalterable as the ancient pyramids in the Andes, everything else, wood, plastic, synthetic all mortal, but concrete blocks immortal. Around the side of the house to the back, down to the basement door, not expecting it to be open, all decided to break in if it wouldn't open, but...eins, zwei, drei and he was in.

Stench. The stench of old wood, old walls, almost like old tobacco, like the stuff he used to (pipe) smoke, cockroaches, one small mouse.

"Hey, don't run away, I'm as harmless as a cigar butt."

But it was 1, 2, 3 gone. He hadn't seen a cigar butt (or pipe) in years, what had ever happened to macho cigars?

Tables, workbenches, scythes, rakes, saws, huge "snipers," watering cans, old iron wheels over against one wall, walking through the basement past piles of old clothes, huge chests, not like his place, all books and computers, walking up creaky stairs to the living room, a sofa, family photos, into the kitchen, an old sloppily-fluffy-haired woman in a long blue-jeanish dress, squinting blue eyes.

"Yeah, your nose is telling the truth, potato dumplings and chicken hearts, gizzards, liver, kidneys, all the good parts ground up into a guess-what-I-am delight. My specialty, you remember, come on in, me boy, you're looking...I was going to say old, but...," laughing, hugging him, feeling it, but was sure something was wrong with his eyes, all those heart and prostate-cancer pills...

"I used to kind of hate winter, you know, nothing to do. But nowadays, I don't care, there's Sammy the dog, he's outside wandering around right now, but in the winter he's inside most of the time. And I love fireplaces and watching Al start the fires. I start things up once in a while. We miss Ireland, but..."

A tall guy wearing a felt cowboy hat, suspenders, farm jeans, comes in, gives him another hug, as if he were feeling it, seeing it, hearing it.

"So I'm glad you could make it. Homestead instead of no-stead," laughing, yet another hug, "Whatever that means....good corn crop this year, and potatoes. No famines here, and wait until you see the pigs, gotta do some smoking pretty soon, but we're set for a long, long winter, and the deer, there's always the deer, the wild turkeys, grouse. I hate the migratory species that desert us every winter."

"So fancy, 'migratory species'!" his mother ridicules him.

"I read a lot, especially in the winter, that's all I learned to do was to read, but...there's country fairs, good book-deals...," motioning for Pat to follow him into the living room, the shelves filled with books, hard-covers, fancy, for a moment feeling he was in some sort of palatial library...

"Why did you ever decide to homestead?"

"It was like going back..."

"Back?"

"Erin go Bragh..."

"I'm afraid I never..."

"Imagine pre-English Ireland, pre-English Scotland, Wales. English history is such a..."

Suddenly a bunch of little girls and guys coming in and all dressed like the nineteenth century, long dresses, short pants, wearing little white inverted cup-cake container hats over quakerish, shakerish long hair, like he'd suddenly walked through a time-barrier he'd always wanted to walk through, back to sanity.

"Come on out, let's go out, you're got to see the mules..."

"And horses."

"The smelly cows."

"Smellier pigs."

Everyone laughing, off in the distance the Montana mountains you could see through the windows.

"Go ahead, no problem, we'll save supper for you all," says Kitchen Grandma.

"Enjoy it while you can!" Mr. Emperor-Farmer of it all, "you ought to see the winter here...but I love it too, the fireplace and everything outside white, rows of corn stubble, like you've never seen sun before...and I still go hunting..."

"Come on! Come on!"

The kiddies screaming, Pat trying to figure out who belonged to him, all the brothers and sisters and kids and grandkids, cousins...

Wavering as he goes out, as if he'd never seen the sky before, a pond in back of the house, endless forests, almost expecting Indians, wouldn't have been surprised if King Solomon walked out of the woods, King Solomon or The Trinity descending, a diamond triangle descending out of the sky, one of the little blondies scream-asking, "So how do you like it?"

"I..."

No words, like he'd never seen clouds before, and a deer off on the edge of the forest.

"I..."

Turning around and then back around and they began to thin out into clouds, mist, their voices becoming thrushes and crows, no more smoke coming out of the chimney, their mist hands waving goodbye and their mist faces sad with loss, back up to the house, empty, no one, no smells, voices.

In the beginning there was nothing and nothing became everything and everything cloud-rained away, down the rivers into the sea of irreversibility.

LINKS

I

Getting old (75), but he still always called his cousins in Chicago, Palos Heights. "Palos" as in sticks...trees...

Hadn't talked to them since the summer before when they'd all come up to Michigan and gone crazy on the lakes.

Rick, the oldest, 78. Ouch! It hurt to even think about it. Like when he'd been in California in October to visit his "soul-mate" best buddy, Gloria, and he'd asked her how old she was and she'd whispered out an almost frightened "Seventy-two...."

Where have all the flowers gone?

Long time passing?

Where have all the flowers gone?

Long time ago.

Got out his phone-book and dialed Rick's number. Rick all alone. Wife dead for, what was it, two, three years? Inoperable brain cancer.

And he'd never picked up with anyone else. Spent most of his time watching TV, a little golf, time with his four brothers and three kids, but the kids were in Seattle (Rick Jr., lawyer), Santa Fe (Marietta, high school teacher) and in Rockford (another daughter, mother of five, wasn't it, which had been her whole life).

Dialed. On the fifth ring Rick answered.

"If this is one of those 'congratulations, I am pleased to inform you that you have just won...'"

Rick as always Mr. Wise Wiseass, but Lou could play the game too.

"This is the Recruiting Assistant Bishop of Chicago, R.A. Bishop Bradbury. We are into the business of recruiting new Catholics due to the recent scandals which have never had or ever will have anything to do with Greater Chicago...including Palatine and Downers' Grove..."

Very ceremonial, stuffy, as Anglo-Irish as he could make it. Rick laughing like crazy.

"Lou! How the hell are you? Springtime-Lou-time...it's been a lonnnng winter. I should have called or written, but I've been so down. Did anyone tell you about my cancer?"

"Not a word, pal!"

Lou's mind suddenly filled with memories/names, images of all his dead friends from recent years, like he was flying over a U.S. graveyard map, Richard Morris in Frisco, Ted Erlandson and Joe Schwartz in L.A., Joe Petrucci in Chicago....

"No cure. Beyond any hope. I'm just taking pills, all swollen up, just waiting to die."

"How come no one told me?"

"They're all depressed. Denial plus mourning, like the stars are talking to

them, 'You're next, all of you, you thought you were immortal, just take a look at Rick, that's all of you in a couple years.' The worst part is that I'm on the younger end of the scale. Maybe it's better if you don't come; all I am these days is..."

"I'll be there tomorrow."

"I can meet you downtown."

"Taxi, no problem."

"But it's way, way out south."

"No problem."

No woman around...the place is a mess..."

"I'll bring a broom, a mop and some soap."

Laughing. How could he manage to laugh into the face of death, but Rich laughed with him, wanted to sign off with an "I love you," but..."

"See you tomorrow, pal."

"Okay, pal, see you tomorrow."

II

Rich was out in Palos Heights, but since Lou's wife's (Mary Anne) death one thing he didn't have to worry about was cash. He had his own retirement money from the university plus her huge M.D. retirement too, the house paid off, the only one living with him his ADD-tortured son, Lou Junior who, at 35, was still deciding his career-goals, two courses a term at Lansing Community College, film or acting or business administration, psychology, cybernetics...another twenty years and he would have taken every course offered, except for the ones in practical stuff like making cars, plumbing, carpetering, house-building...for him the more theoretical the better.

Lou stepping out of the main airport building at O'Hare, flagging down a cab, and, as he expected, a black-black guy was at the wheel. Super-tall, thin.

"Palos Heights!"

"You mean THE Palos Heights?"

"Yeah, I've got the address written down," pulling one of his little notebooks out of the inside pocket of his English tweed suit-coat, his usual, "all the details as we how to get there."

"You're the boss. It's gonna cost!"

"No problem. I'll love to have a little time with a Sudanese."

Starting out, then pulling back to the curb.

"How do you know I'm Sudanese? Do you work for the FBI or something? I'm straight, man, straight as the Tribune Tower."

"And just as gothic!" laughed Lou.

"Whatever you say, man, God-who?"

"Goth-ic! Like medieval."

You'd be surprised, Sudan isn't all that primitive, lots of problems, but once people get out..."

Lou almost saying "They end up driving cabs," but didn't.

"You're doing fine!"

"I've got one son going to Northwestern...cybernetics...and a daughter in nursing."

"You're not that old! Come on!"

"Too old, that's the way I always feel. How come sea-turtles live three hundred years and we only live, I was going to say a hundred...I wouldn't mind a hundred."

"Your English is great!"

"I watch a lot of TV; listen to a lot of talk-shows on the radio while I've waiting for guys like you."

"I'd like to go to Africa some time, that's the one place I've never been."

"You don't have to, Africa's coming here."

"Great with me. There's such a difference between Africans and..."

"There wasn't such a difference when the slaves first came over, but society stripped them of all their tribalness, languages, religions, turned them into pet dogs..."

"Worse than that. Almost free labor."

"Sometimes I feel like going back, or getting bleached and surgeonified, turn into an Irishman."

"The same thing happened to Irishmen in a way...Americanization..."

"It'd be fun to go back a hundred years."

"A few thousand."

"How about a hundred into the future...the 'blackification' of America!"

"Could be..."

On the highway now, the serious super-crowded highway.

"Listen, if you're ever up in Michigan," Lou reaching into the upper left pocket of his Harris tweed jacket, getting out a little notebook he used to write poetry in, writing his name and stuff on a blank sheet, handing it to him.

"Here's my name, address, phone, e-mail."

The driver taking it.

"How about your blood type? A little DNA?"

"You're good...great gringofication!"

"Gringofi-what?"

"Gringo as in non-Latino...non..."

"Non-native....I know lots of Latinos in Chicago, and let me tell it, not very often I enjoy 'customers,' usually they just, I was going to say 'grin and bear it,' but it's more like 'grim and bear it.'"

"You're amazing...your English."

"Well, I went to English schools."

"Tell me more about them."

And Lou sat back a little, hoping the ride would be longer than he knew it

would be, no matter what the cost. Or maybe once they got out to the Heights they could stop and have a beer...a break...missing his students, hating retirement, missing his Africans and Orientals, the Croatians and Czechs and Bavarians...English for Foreign Students...if he could he would start all over again, twenty-five, ON YOUR MARK, READY TO GO...always ready to go anywhere but R.I.P.

III

Up to the front door, 222 W. Amarillo Street, which Lou thought was a weird Hispanic name for a Chicago suburb.

Waved goodbye to his Sudanese friend, home addresses, e-mails exchanged, a beginning, not an end, Lou feeling he needed new contacts/explorations in his old days...years...hoping for as many as he could get. The voices inside him always whispering "Don't think about death, think about potato soup and nice legs at the table next to you as you sip your hazelnut decafe and eat your opium poppy seed muffins...now, now, now, wow, wow, wow...."

"A bientôt!"

One more wave goodbye. Amazed at how good Sudanese Rudolph's English and French were....

Reaching forward and pushing hard on the bell. Chimes, deep, resonant chimes. Very nice.

No response.

Rang again. And again. And again. Waited patiently, his mind starting in again, "He's dead, you got here too late...or if not dead out on a date, not funny..," started counting the number of times he pushed the button, 11...12...on the 13th ring Rick cumbersomely and lugubriously opening the door, propped up on a walker.

"I'm sorry, I..."

Rick managing to squeeze through the opening without knocking Rick down. But barely. Rick a blown-up balloon, Mr. Thin Man all "expanded" and swollen, Rick watching Lou watching him.

"It's the cancer...and the medicine. It looks like I'm just waiting to explode, nicht wahr?"

"Nicht wahr?"

"'Isn't it true?' That's all it means."

"I know what it means....how long do they say you've got?"

"A maximum of six months."

"Nothing can be done?"

"It's all over. Maybe in the future, chemotherapy...who knows. They may learn how to make people last five hundred years like sea-turtles, but now...and no one comes around...dead wife, brothers and sisters and kids and grandkids, cousins, old girlfriends from way back...I depress everyone...everyone vanishes politely...oh, so politely. It's a 1932 film. But the faces don't fool me. You'll

probably leave at dawn."

Walking into the living room where he cumbersomely sits

down on the sofa in front of the huge, luxurious TV, Lou sitting down on a chair under an oversize photo of the family, maybe 30, 40 years old while Rick's parents were still around, Lou's mother, Rick's father's sister, that's where the link was, everyone in the picture there for a Christmas party family get-together, Rick's four brothers and one sister, Lou himself a painfully only child, seeing the picture Lou suddenly missing his grandmother and grandfather (who weren't invited to Rick's parents' place for anything) his dead friends, what in lilac's' name was with TIME? Why couldn't life be a couple of thousand years, or just forever like the...nothing was forever was it, not even the stars...

"I may end up in a hospice soon, soon, soon."

"We'll see, but in the meantime..."

"In the meantime what about a little news?" Turning on the TV. The evening news.

Robberies, murders, pictures of old neighborhoods he was familiar with, where he grew up, the far South Side, down in Hyde Park where he used to go to this Catholic bookstore and buy Gilbert Keith Chesterton and Evelyn Waugh (Brideshead Revisited), lots of commercials about erection-stimulators and sleeping pills, previews of the most unsexy TV series he'd ever seen, Sex in the City...

Then the weather report, the cold spring continuing: "The coldest spring in
seventy-five years..."

Rich finally switching over to the movie channels, some Jimmy Stewart film about the wild west, Lou laughing, "Did you ever stop to think that we were born before TV, before refrigerators, furnaces, computers, cell-phones...I mean we were pretty primitive..."

"I liked it that way. Look at it now...and all the work to create unions, and everything made in China...no one word about closing down steel mills and clothes manufacturing factories, refrigerator factories..."

Rich turning down the sound.

"No, don't turn it down."

"How about it OFF?" Another Click and Rick yawned, "Sometimes I think I could just sleep all day and all night, just wake up to eat, crap, piss...that how lazy I'm getting."

"Me too...only then when it's time to sleep, I can't"

"Here, let me give you a little touch of Irish Creme."

Going into a large, beautifully conservative, nineteenth century English-looking armoire in the corner, opening it, filled with bottles of all sorts of exotica, taking out a little "jug" of Irish Creme and finding two glasses in one corner of the top shelf, again the glasses all "shaped" and decorated, cut full of designs, half filled the glasses, emptied the jug, handed one glass to Rick and clicked his against Rick's, whispering "Bon chance!"

Lou answering him back, "Bon chance!" both of them downing the Irish
Crème in one gulp." So you speak a little French, huh?"

"Fluent . Studied here, then vacations in Paris and in the south of France. You know, Le Massif Central."

"Sure...where thousands of years ago the primitives would scare animals to jump off the top and kill themselves..."

"Laura loved France. And my job at Ford."

"Accountant?"

"CFO."

"Pardon my ignorance, but..."

"Chief Financial Officer. It took me all over the place. Alienated my brothers a little. There they were SOXING like maniacs, and I'd soccer it up with international scores...I remember Mack one time, half-kidding, half-not, 'If everyone followed your lead it'd be the end of the whole U.S. sports world,'" Rick pulling back the covers a little, revealing rich sheets, everything as fresh as a fresh cut loaf of old time bread, then sitting down on a chair next to the bed, obviously overjoyed at having Lou on board The Good Ship More Than Enough, going into an old antiques cabinet next to the chair, taking out two small flower-decorated crystal glasses, pulling out another jug of Irish Crème liquor...

"We -- I -- never run out around here. Just a little more nightcap. Sedative, a ride on the Good Ship Lollisleep!"

"Sounds good to me," Lou agreeing, "My favorite drink in the world."

Rick lifting up his glass for a click, Lou responding, clicking.

"Erin go brough!"

"Erin go brough!"

"No forgetting roots," Rick sipping slowly, slowly, slowly, "You know what Id' really like to do, now that I'm both a widower and retired? Go back in time, or find a place that's itself back in time, some valley, village, like Athenry in Ireland or, you know, that place where Pagnol grew up in southern France, Ma Vlast Bohemia..."

"Ma Vlast?"

"My country. Czech. One of Dvorak's greatest pieces, 'In Bohemia's Meadows and Forests.' And I love Lili Boulanger too, don't you? What about our grandfather who homesteaded in Montana. I wouldn't mind trying there...Giverney, a nice Monet landscape...."

"Wait a minute, what's all this Dvorak, Boulanger, Pagnol? You're supposed to be the big football fan family, football, baseball, hockey, golf, wrestling...you name it...none of this French-Czech stuff. Next thing you'll be singing Mahler!"

Rick suddenly becoming a pillar of solemnity, like he'd never seen anyone in his family -- the perpetual making-fun-of-everything jokers -- before, starting to sing.

"Wir geniessen der himlischen Freuden,
Drum tun wir das Irdische merden,
Kein weltlich Getünmel...."

On and on. Turning the original soprano into bass, but Lou hardly cared.

All the way down to "Die Englein, die buchen, das Brot...."

Lou translating the last line, "'The angels break the bread.' Mahler's 4th Symphony."

"I just wish I believed in himmlischen freuden."

Rich, translating again.

"Heavenly delights. I don't think we're cousins at all, but two chips off the same log, two antennae on the same firefly..."

"Two chips in the same cookie...chocolate chips, I mean..."

Both of them cracking up with laughter, an embrace.

"Zeit zu schlafen."

"Time to sleep."

And Rick started on his way out the door.

"You'll be okay, no sleeping pills?"

"The Irish Creme'll do it."

"Okay, pal, and sleep well. Thanks for being here, should I close the door?"

"Leave it open a crack, a crack the size of an elephant's tusk."

"The size of my swollen legs..."

And he's gone, Lou going into the John for one last leak. One last drop into a Kleenex.

Into bed.

So many sleepless nights, getting up every couple hours as his bladder began to whisper "Now, now again!," wondering how long both of them/either of them would be above ground. But he'd stay until Rick "left," although you never knew who might be going first.

Too short!

Too many oaks and sycamores, les jambs/legs, Puccini arias, little Mother Goose suites and unknown French impressionists

(Pissaro), too many Garbo and Hepburn films to see, Wim Wenders and Pagnol, Les Demoiselles D'Avignon...

Maybe a little under-the-tongue Melatonin wouldn't hurt, got up and got one out of his bag. Before he started to remember names...Chicago symphony concerts always on Saturday nights, a box seat, with gorgeous pianist-to-be (she eventually became a lawyer) Dolores Volini, his German professor at Loyola always a couple of boxes down, and he'd always wave hello, and when the conductor would come out he'd always give a special wave to big shot Czech-exile Schwartzenberg professor...such a life he'd had growing up in Chicago, violin and piano and paint/paint-brushes, a little Ich liebe dich wie du liebst mich/ I love you as you love me, his Viennese opera teacher, his ample little Czech (Yaksa Mash?/How are you?) grandmother, then later falling in love with Yvette, studying art at the Art Institute in Chicago, six kids, always visiting the family in Lyonnais...

Stretching out.

As I lay me down to sleep,
crowds of angels o'er me keep....

Or was it weep?

Mendelssohn's Elijah? Or Hansel and Gretel? Or...or....or...

He couldn't remember anything anymore, could barely recognize Sibelius' Finlandia or Grieg's Norwegian dances, or would mix them together....

Carmina Burana by Karl...? Orf! Sometimes it came.

The only thing he never ever forgot (Adolph Menjou in Stage Door with Veronica Lake...and he'd loved that latest English Pride and Prejudice film, never checked the names of the actors and actresses, the ultimate sanity, enjoy, enjoy, enjoy, no questions asked) was

HUGH FOX

REQUIEST IN
SHALOM, SHALOM, SHALOM
PEACE.

SHHHHHHHHHH

My God, this is in the middle of nowhere, and I mean Nowhere," he said after they'd turned off Bitterroot Road to Lagrima Read. Dirt now, nice and muddy-splashy from the Spring rain, "maybe we ought to come back in the summer when it's drier..."

"It's never drier here from what I've read," she answered, opening the window, actually enjoying the Spring wind, "it's delicious, really...and look at all the flowers. No hint when it comes to names, except for the dandelions..."

"No hibiscus here," he smiled, road bumpy too, sometimes having to slow down to avoid a fallen tree, passing a flattened-down barn and tottering old wooden farmhouses, "Look at that. I wonder how many years ago that was built...and abandoned...how long ago was your family place built?"

"Nineteen hundred."

"Three hundred and seven years ago. And when was The Obliteration?"

"There were various New York, Pittsburg, Minneapolis, Denver. But they didn't get out into the countryside until about 2100..."

"And what did they do here?"

"Stories get passed down, but I guess it was mainly beef, corn, hay. I don't know, it all sounded so primitive as the stories got passed down. Thank Allah that
they still let us speak English!"

"English okay, but I like it out here, even without mosques."

"They lived on the edge of a river, the Looking Glass River. Three kilometers from the beginning of the road we're on, in fact..."

Then up ahead of them was a river, the bridge out so they couldn't go any further, on the edge of the river the ruins of an ancient red-brick house, two stories, a widow's watch on top, ruined front porch and steps, lots of the bricks "unscaling," falling into bits and scraps, but...

"I love it," he said, "my ancestors were from Chicago and they used to always see Michigan as Kingdom Come...," pulling to a stop and scrambling up the fragmented steps walking up to the broken-down door, pulled off its hinges, still a trace of white pain on its fragments, "You know, before the final bombing. Weird how the Water Tower survived, survived the Chicago Fire, then Armageddon..."

"I wouldn't mind living here," she said, "we could grow our own crops, have sheep, chickens, cattle, grow corn. Look, there's the fragment of an apple orchard, imagine how they used to live out here before cars, what seemed like a million miles from any town. Save your turnips and cabbages, parsnips, potatoes in the fall, some chickens for eggs, some to eat. I don't know when they invented canned and bottle goods, but they had bottled jams and things, no electricity,
radios, TV, computers, candles, fireplaces, long winter nights, long summer days, isolation, Mom and Dad and the kids and summer and winter solstices, Jesus in His heaven and ..."

She starts to cry, they walk into the doorless house, she stands next to a windowless window looking out, a single deer chomping away at the grass, and then two baby deer...

"What about germ-warfare and HIV and radioactivity, the virus clouds, some of that stuff may have survived."

"Come on, look outside, venison, Nature is self-cleaning, restorative, it's man who..."

He puts his hand over his mouth.

"Maybe we could stay here tonight, or come back with blankets, fix the chimney, there's all kinds of wood outside. We don't even need windows, turn it into a cave, escape the...," she stop, stretches out on the irregular, super-weathered worn-out carpet on the oak floor, "escape the..."

"Shhhh...no need to specify," and he lies down uncomfortably next to her, both of them imagining chairs, sofas, beds, seasons, solstices, la vie primitif, as if France and the rest of it out there still existed.

IMMORTAL JAGUAR

Once you got outside of La Paz it was all dirt roads. Hardly roads at all, just ribbons of potholed confusion winding through wilderness. Instant time-travel back to the pre-historic. Which in a way was perfect -- one way to prevent the destruction of the millennial cultures that still inhabited the altiplano almost untouched and unchanged by the disease of The Modern.

"Okay, see you later!" I said to Carmen and gave her a hug and a kiss, kissed and hugged the mother, Socorro, the almost invisible little Indian maid, with most of her teeth gone in front, a couple molars left for grinding her food. You would have thought that Carmen and Mariano would have gotten her some false teeth, but, of course, it may have occurred to me, it never would have occurred to them. There was "us" and "them." We were to be served; they were to serve. The mentality of the Conquista still alive and well

It was only supposed to be a day's outing but, somehow, I knew better, knew that I would never see them again -- at least in this life. Other lives...? I wasn't sure.

It was a long drive out of the city to Tiawanaku and just as rough as I had expected. There were a couple of times when we hit potholes that would have broken the axles of lesser vehicles.

"There's this old priest living out with the Indians, about an hour beyond Tiawanaku. He is said to be a miracle-worker, preaching a new gospel for a new age. The perfect subject for a feature article, and who knows where it can go from here. Can't you just imagine picking up a copy of Paris Match and there's the article in French, my byline and all...?"

"Why not?" I answered.

It was true enough; the world out there was hungry for any kind of spiritual message to fill its spiritual emptiness.

I dipped into my pocket and hunted up a few Datura seeds, started chewing on them. Speaking of spiritual emptiness...

"It's fun for me to get out and see a little of the real world," said Ricardo, "mainly all I do is take pictures of corpses, brides, bridegrooms and newborn infants, births, Baptisms, First Communions, weddings, The Dead...no one ever seems to want pictures of divorces..."

Ha, ha, ha, ha....

They seemed like a perfect couple, like two pairs of old shoes thrown into an old suitcase together.

It must have taken an hour to get to the ruins themselves and they let us off next to a kind of crude, improvised restaurant/refreshment stand close to the entrance.

"So, listen, we'll be back by about five, how's that?" said Maria del Carmen, "there'll be a little light left. And anyhow, Ricardo has wonderful night vision. They don't call him El Lobo [the Wolf] for nothing."

"So we'll meet you right here!" said Ricardo, pointing to the restaurant/refreshment stand.

And there we were, left by ourselves as the jeep bumped off down the road into still more remote No Man's Lands.

"I feel depressed," said Alex as we made our way into the ruins themselves.

"Me too," I admitted, walking past gigantic slabs of beautifully worked stone all tumbled and broken. Not just ruins but pillaged ruins, for centuries used as a stone quarry to build churches like the Catholic Church at Copacabana, stone for railroad bridges, stone for buildings in La Paz. It was as if the great pyramids in Egypt had been dismantled in order to build Cairo.

I couldn't help but cry, put my arm around Alex as I walked into the ruins and saw what Ponce Sanginés and his crew had done to add insult to injury, reassembling the stone, putting drains up where there was nothing to drain, assembling stones the way they had never been assembled before, in my own mind slowly the ruins becoming what they were, a steady hum inside me, choirs of eagles and jaguars filling my mind, looking at The City That Had Been, all covered with gold-plate, shining in the sacred sun, walking up to the top of the Akapana, Mount Illimani to my left, calling to me with its gigantic thunder-voice in the sky, "Tinku, tinquichi....the place of the encuentro/encounter...this is where you must come to reconcile all oppositions...through Achuma to the Land of the Achacillas...come home to your beginnings which are the seeds of all our possible futures..."

Words swirling through me.

The Aymara Tinku like the Hebrew Tikun , Tikun Olam, The Order of the World....through the mind-opening road of the hallucinogenic cactus Achuma to the Land of the Achachillas, the Grandfathers/Ancestors...

"This is the Sacred Center, Nacan, Annaka, Nax, the center, core, belly, belly-botton of the world...you have come home to your beginnings, which are also all your possible futures..."

The ombligo, umbilical center of the world, Quiché Maya surging through me, the ancient pre-Columbian languages of Haiti and the Guayanas, fragments of ideas/words left behind by the ancient pilgrims on their way to the world-center.

"Chuki, the Land of Gold, the gold-sky and golden land..."

Chukiyawu, the original name for La Paz...standing there everything beginning to shine, all restored and clothed in gold again, the waters of the fountains flowing out of their artfully constructed basins, a water falling spout dropping into a basin that flowed underground again, emerging again into the sunlight, then underground, out, in, over and over again, the magic fountains described on the way to the Land of the Sun King in The Odyssey, which were really descriptions of the Sun King's Land itself, faintly remembered, passed down generation after generation, fragmentary memories of voyages from Anatolia to here, the world-mountain/world-center, filtering into ancient Greece from a so much more ancient world in Asia Minor.

"Pacha ,world, space, final judgment, Taypi, center, cola, stone...," the voices changing, 'condensing' only into her voice, "Now you shall become one with Pachamama, the great Earth as Mother, Mother of us All, you and I one with the earth that is one with the sky, at the moment of rebirth after temporary death..."

I don't know how much Alexandra understood, could even 'hear' of the voices swirling around us. But I did feel she was inside the vision, standing there crying along with me...seeing as I saw, everything differently, a puma carved into a wall the image of the shamanic transformation I (we) had undergone. Herakles/Hercules again. The fanged god fanged because he had become divine.

Bird-snakes coming out of the top of his head, the uniting of sky (quetzal) and earth (coatl-snake)...the Aztec coatl a combination of "co" as in "container" and "atl," water, so that all the fountained play of water here around us and in minds became a play of the Great Snake Mother mating with Father Sky at this moment of maximum death and resurrection...

Everything "spoke" to me.

The belly-button of the central figure on the sun-gate behind which the sun would rise the next morning on the day of the Winter Solstice.The calendrical-astronomical jaguar sun-god year-carrier from whose belly-button sprouted two more bird-fish, another fish twisted, lying on top of the central sun-symbol that I alone had seen for what it was, although it was the most obvious thing in the world, once you knew Indus Valley, Brahmi, Sumerian scripts. The deltas on the fish itself, doors opening into the infinite horizon of sacred apple-induced visions...the same motif repeated again and again, all over the giant stone statue called Kochamama.

NAGA (Sanskrit), NAKU (Sumerian),

NAKASH (Hebrew),
NABA-ROA (Guarao), Nawach (Hopi)...

Water, water-serpents, the serpent in this, the original Garden of Eden, not evil as pictured in the bible, but the source of all fertility and joy. This was my spiritual home and I understood every jaguar- and condor-head, every little Garudaish year-bearing bird.Osiris, the sun-god man-bird. The Assyrian god Assur crossing the sky in a winged disk.

We wandered through the ruins for hours, time slowly running out for me, like sand through an hour glass. Alex knew what was coming. She was almost as much a shaman as I, and when I turned to her toward the end of the day, about to say it was time for me to go on alone now, to the cave world that had its entrance at the base of Mount Illimani, that she should wait for Ricardo and Maria del Carmen at the restaurant/refreshment stand where they said they would meet us, she already had read my thoughts and her answer was simply "Take me with you."

"No, you have all your life ahead of you, all I have is Past. It hardly makes any difference for me now, there is so little left. I am the prisoner of inevitability."

"You know how much I love you..."

"And how much I love you. Which is why I can't take you with me."

One last glance back at the old sun-god, Helios, carrying the two bird-snakes of the year in his hands.

I walked her back to the entrance, looked up overhead where the seven-headed serpent Losun/Ladon (Portuguese Latão-tin) would (what the Occident knew as the Pleiades) soon appear.

Of all my children, Alexandra in all her restlessness and creativity, intuitiveness, idealism, innocence, was the most like me.

"So what's going to happen to you?" she asked, "When will

I see you again?"

"If I only knew..."

"Why are you doing this?"

"Do you believe that The Immortals have died?" I asked.

"Not really," she answered, sweeping the sad, despoiled ruins with her gaze, from horizon to horizon, scanning, imprinting it all on her soul, "they're still here in a way...almost erased...just traces left...but still here..."

"And you can hear what's out there, can't you?" I asked, turning toward Mount Illimani, the world-mountain, the original Intihuatana, The Place Where the Sun is Tied, every Inca ruin having a monolithic stone-post solstice-stone that was a pale, miniaturized replica of Mount Illimani itself.

She stood next to me facing Mount Illimani.

What I heard was a great roar, like a waterfall, pounding surf, jaguar growls, beckoning me. This was the night of the Descent into the Underworld, my personal Good (Bad) Friday when I would have to descend into Hell, die and be dismembered yet again. The year died; my own personal life replicated the cyclic birth-death rhythms of the stars.

I reached into my pocket and gave her all the money I had with me.

No last will, no testament. Everything was in order. She had her return ticket to the U.S.; it was just a question of taking her to the airport. Most of the flights from Bolivia were half-empty anyhow, you never had to worry about reservations.

"So long, pal," I said, turned and started to walk in the direction of Thunder and Lightning Mountain.

I could hear her calling to me "Dad, Dad, Dad," but I didn't (couldn't) look back, just kept walking across the desolate landscape until I couldn't hear her any longer.

It was the end of scholarship for me now, little scholarly insights, links, correlations, dictionaries, walking into Sumerian and Akkadian, back through Tamil and Gond to proto-Dravidian, using Hebrew as a handy wrench to open up locked doors of the past. The end of museums, Cairo, Tunis, Mohenjo Daro, Harrapa, La Paz,Chicago.Visits to other sites that touched on, fed into this ultimate, final Home of the Gods -- Ugarit, Çatak Hüyük, the rock reliefs at Yazilikaya, the lion gates at Hattusas that were faint echoes of their counterparts at Tiawanaku, Ur and Khafajeh, Ain Ghazal, Mari, Nimrud, Uruk, Babylon....

The Taurus Mountains flowed through me now. I was drifting down the Euphrates past Akkad and Sumer, remembering the letter from Rib-Adda of Byblos to Amenophis IV, speaking of "The Great King...my Lord...the Sun-God..."

I was there now, the Allpast flowing through me, cold, hungry (I should have taken some food with me, but, of course, I didn't), my heart beating twice its normal speed, wanting to just lie down and give up, wait for the Angel of Death to find me in the midst of all this rocky, dead desolation.

Too much wind, too much dust and dryness. And for every step I took forward it seemed like I had taken a step back, Illimani itself instead of growing larger as I advanced toward it, shrinking, diminishing down to nothingness.

The sun on the edge of the horizon now.

Ricardo and Maria del Carmen would have picked up Alex by now and they would have been all talking about what they should do. Should they come after me? Go the police? Get help? Or just let me alone to my own devices and destiny?

Let me alone.

A shadow walking next to me now, with every step becoming a little more solid, at first amorphous and vague, but gradually assuming form, both our shadows at their ultimate lengthening now as the sun went down below the horizon, two jaguars/pumas, surrounded by our still-coalescing, form-taking peers, duplicating the rituals of prehistory, everyone coming now to the world-center, every tribe, messenger, angel-demon, bird-soul, cat-soul, all the languages of the world flowing through me, Tiawanaku, Tiwatinaku, Torikaminotake, Mount Kunlun, the land of the Washu/Wanaku, Kahuna where Wanadi (Wanaku) the sun-god lives...

A short dusk after sunset.

The vulture-king out of Guarajo myth was waiting for us, the sun-king with gilded human skins (Diodorus Siculus) in his closet, He Who Never Dies, living in the midst of the deathless, praying to myself "Vishnu, Vishnu do not wake now and destroy us, we who are your dream."

Feeling more and more "tenuous", cloudlike, unfleshed, my own jaguar-companion totally with me now as the moon rose and the landscape was platinized, silver-plated and we rolled together in the spirit-world like two spiraling tendrils of pure erotic energy.

She gave me some small fleshy "buttons" to eat -- which I ate, and the landscape became as red as blood and the two of us, my ageless lady and I swirled and swirled again together into orgasmic splicings of the purest joy.

Still walking, advancing on the mountain, surrounded by The Dead now, my father, not as I last saw him, heavy and sad, after his final heart attack, simply waiting to die, but young and idealistic, the gypsy violinist I had never known, my mother as I had never known her, daisy fields of exuberance, my dead brother, Noah, grown now, although he had died (meningitis) when he was only two, abrazos, abrazos and more abrazos, Phyllis Miller, who had been mutilated beyond recognition in a car crash when she was twenty-five, coming toward me restored and more than restored, "You know I always loved you," "And I you," Jackie Eubanks, funny and big and bouncy as always, wizened, philosopher-eyed Sidney Bernard and the great Kaballist, my spiritual mentor, Menke Katz.

"I told you it would be this way!!" he shouted, hands up like a referee calling a touchdown/goal, singing Shalom Aleichem the way he always sang it, only he himself an angel now, or a close (eternal) cousin...

Then I looked again and they were all skulls, it was an army of skeletons marching toward the mouth of Hell, the landscape littered with bones, phantom vultures diving down and carrying bones away. Prometheus at night being devoured before his restoration the following dawn.

And who was I in the midst of all this drama of death and resurrection, crucified on the cross of my own ignorance and "newness" to the game?

I was the voyager from across the sea, wasn't I, the one who had passed through the endless mind-zodiac puzzles of the last forty years of scholarship that everyone had said was wasted time ("No more books about Tiawanaku, please" -- Al Silverstein, Prince of New York Agents), clashing gates and scorpion claws, lions and crabs and vultures, my whole life a tortured tumbling through the zodiac-vortex of the years...

I was Prometheus, Odysseus, Herakles, Gilgamesh, Jason, Susanawo come at last to the World Mountain, Mashu, Meru, to die...and be reborn...

In Germanic myth Hel is the goddess who lives at the base of the world-mountain where Valhalla is on top, the Home of the Gods. And in German "hel" is light, not darkness, like Helios the sun....

HEL
HELIOS

So that the sun-king and the goddess of the underworld merge, the Minotaur at the end of the (zodiac?) labyrinth, the sun-bull-man who emerges from Hell at the end /beginning of the solar year.

159

Where had Time gone to? I wondered as the sun (Hel/Helios) began to lighten the sky behind the World Mountain. Of course there was a resurrection. Of course there would be a New Covenant, a New Earth, a Second and a Third, an endless succession of Re-Comings. And the Holy Spirit wasn't just in us, but we were holy spirits ourselves now...as the sun came up over Illimani and we approached the mouth of the cave beneath it, heard the flow of the holy river inside and saw the gold, bull-headed Yama-god of the Underworld-New Sun emerge and walk directly toward us...

"It's so nice you got the day off," she said as she pulled into downtown Westin and found a parking spot right in the same block with the stores and restaurants, "Don't you love it here?"

"Question number one first," he answered all lawyerly, although he wasn't a lawyer at all but a rare-books/weird books librarian at UMKC, "The day off, I took it off, I didn't get it off. I hate July days off, April is more like it...," getting out of the car, wearing his Harris tweeds and smoking a meerschom pipe, Mixture 49, his boss always telling him, "You look like 1950...and that might even be 1950 B.C.!"

"There's this winery-brewery up the street, goofy name, beautiful place, Pirtle, that's been turned into a restaurant," she said, burping a long burp, four months pregnant, "Excuse Burpy Me...it's enough to cancel out the pregnancy..."

"You'll be fine, it's just the first few months, I've been reading up on it on the internet."

"It's getting to be like living in a sci-fi movie, not 'pass me the pancakes,' but 'pass me my I-pod...'"

"I wanna be a father-grandfather...multiple times..."

"Once is enough and then some."

"Wait until you see the baby."

She burps again, like she's been drinking beer and eating onion rings all morning, suddenly gets very 'businessy,' "Listen, I'll be one hour. I can walk from here. Thirteen thirteen Locust Street. I hate the two thirteens together, like double-whammy bad luck...and the family's kind of the same way, this nine year old who's totally down in the dumps. 'Everyone wants to kill me at school. And at home. Nobody likes the way I look, I'm too small, a real runt, that's what they call me, and too Irish-looking, they all hate the Irish. I don't drink but everyone calls me a drunk. I wanna go to another school, another planet. Everyone wants to kill me. Can't you find me a UFO somewhere to take me to another planet...?'"

"Sounds pretty imaginative to me," he starts walking along with her, up toward the winery, the river right next to the whole downtown, river and trees...

"Don't you just love it here?" She's all turned on, he's never seen her so 'herself,' exuberant, out-going, involved with the world around her. Usually she's the incarnation of self- involvement, not that he's that different, "What I love about these little towns --I almost said 'townling' as in 'deerling,' if even that's right -- I mean the rivers, they always build next to rivers and they always have park-space, walk-around space...it's so old-worldish, I don't know, like the time I went to southern France and Monet's place at Giverny...the people are always so open, not defensive like in the city, no gangs, drugs, all that, I feel sorry I ever stopped painting, like I'd like to go to Provence, all this war-stuff and murdering stuff...know you what I mean?"

"You ought go back into art."

"Not with five hundred a month to pay, my tuition debts."

"Who knows, you could make big money as a painter. When I look at the piles of your paintings, wood-carvings, etchings, drawings, in the garage, I always wanna take them and fill the house with um. They're top drawer. All the clowns and the river scenes, the downtown Kansas City warehouses, parks, farm-fields, everything you touch is magic, you're like a combination of Rembrandt, Picasso, Renoir and Dali."

"Not Dali!"

"Dollie! Dolly Parton!" He laughs, she doesn't. "Sorry," getting stone-cold serious now, "I'm telling you, when I go to the Nelson Gallery and see the French impressionists it's like seeing your work. You're a maniac when it comes to nature."

"What I love about towns like this, okay, it's frogs and

racoons, minnows and trout, lilac bushes and multi-colored leaf-shows every Fall, but…" her voice lowering, secrets to tell that she didn't want anyone else but him to hear. "There are no sects. It's all one tribe, one everything, one language, one menu, belief…differences are what screw everything up. But here, look around, it's pure, if you'll pardon the term, 'hick-shit' oneness…."

"No, I won't pardon the word. I feel like one of the crowd here."

"So do I. That's what I mean."

And it was true, you looked around and it was all the same eyes, jaws, glasses, no glasses, shoes, drawls, onenesses.

"The worst thing that ever happened was tribalness. Bible A versus Bible B, the Amorites versus the Jews…"

"Amorites?"

"One of those 'enemy' tribes that the bible says God helped the Jews defeat. There could be a million little unrelated-to-each-other territories."

"Or how about everyone intermarrying with everyone else, make it a worldwide salad bar?"

They were in front of the old German winery now. She played traffic-cop and stopped him.

"So you stay here. I'll be back as soon as I can (another big burp)…sometimes I wish…"

"You'd had the baby yesterday?"

"Never mind."

"Sometimes you wish WHAT? Come on! No secrets!"

She starts walking away; up the hill to where she has to do her counseling. He follows her.

"I gotta go."

"Come on!"

He's on the edge of fury, steps in front of her, blocks her way.

"You wanna see what I learned in Karate class?"

"What happened to your Kansas accent?"

"I'm from the Bronx, right now. You wanta sample?"

Suddenly he softens, tears in his eyes. Steps back to let her pass, but she doesn't, stands there all confused, just over to the edge of tears too.

"I keep thinking/dreaming about Monet in Giverny. Van Gogh, you know, Pissaro, Picasso, Renoir, Renoir's son, Le Petite Dejeuner Sur L'Herbes, Marguerite Duras, Lili Boulanger..."

"Wai...wai...wait...Lili Boulanger?"

"French composer, died when she was twenty-four. Fauré taught her composition when she was a kid."

"What happened to painting?"

"All the arts...all it is is taking the shields and armour off Reality, seeing what's really there...reality lessons...l'eternité...la mer mélée au soleil..."

"What a minute. Eternity...the sea mixed with the soul...."

"The sun...soleil...," crying now, handkerchief out, she kisses him, all solemnly...and leaves, "See you in about an hour."

He goes on to the deck, orders a beer, dark Malt German, takes a notebook out of his pocket and begins to draw the trees, gulch, gulley, stream in front of him, the forest. A notebook he'd bought for her and if she saw what he could do with a little pencil-magic...

ESSENCES

"I'll tell ya," said Dr. Montrose as solemnly dictatorial as Tupin talking about the ex-/future Russian empire, "we can take your brain, enclose it in a life-support system, no eyes, tongue, taste, ears...just the brain itself, no present or future, just memory/dreams...."

Albrecht suddenly getting all teary-eyed sentimental, "Fall along the Seine, boating up the Thames, visiting Glenna in Carpinteria..."

"Carpinter-what? What are you talking about?"

"Carpinteria, she and her husband have this place on the California coast. In love for fifty years but we never touched each other, a portrait of her over the fireplace when she was fifteen, like a blonde water lily in a blue dress..."

Dr. Montrose smiles.

"I like that. That was at seventeen. Now what's she like fifty years later?"

"Not fifty years later, sixty seven years later. She's seventy-two...."

"Maybe we could put her brain next to yours. If there were some way to connect them..."

"How long will it last? I mean the brain, our brains?"

"It's hard to say, out of the body and all, all kind of revivifying agents. I spent twenty years in Santiago de Chile in Ecuador in the mountains where living to a hundred and twenty was very common. You know, the Apples of Immortality. Wagner's Freya..."

"I don't know what you're talking about."

"I just hope I do. Our swine have done beautifully, our pheasants and dogs..."

"You mean I can be immortal? Immortal in a hospital."

"2010, 2050, 2100....will there be any hospitals left? What I'm thinking about first is hospitalization-stabilization, then, what's her name, Amy, your M.D. wife's daughter in Kansas City, your wife's not going to be around very long I guess, she oughta be here today, but your daughter...you can be a living heirloom in her home in Kansas City and then her daughter or son...nothing wrong with being a living heirloom..."

"And power outages?"

"We can build in a self-generator, just small technical details."

"Generation after generation after generation?"

"As long as you last. Or maybe you'd rather have your wife's brain next to you instead of Glenna's. Or maybe both of them. A menage a trois...I've been so boringly one wife, one life..."

"But how will you know when I'm gone?"

"All kinds of built-in alarm systems."

"But, really, what if my cancers got into my brain?"

"I doubt they will, without the rest of your body, no carcinogenic stimuli. Of course there's bound to be some degeneration, but I'm not promising immortality, just extended mortality."

"I keep thinking of Glenna out in Santa Barbara. Couldn't you attach our brains to computerized bodies, or even bodiless just attach us so we can dream together?"

"Not ready for that yet. We're not ready for other solar systems yet, some day, perhaps, but...you can dream about her all you want for as long as you've got..."

"You should have seen that portrait of her as a young sylph! And the years of daily e-mails, soul-mates, that's what she always called us, what she always wrote about. I'd fly out to see her every once in a while, was good pals with her husband too, and when he died I wanted to just go out there and be with her full-time..."

"And what happened?"

"I don't know. She's like all my old -- and I mean OLD -- friends. All she thinks about is death. Like she's already dead."

"So you don't want a menage a trois brain-triangle, three brains next to each other, maybe, just maybe not even connected."

Albrecht gets up, leaning on is cane. It's a real struggle; he's almost tottering over to his doom, one big bang on his drum-head and that's the end of Symphony Number End.

"So what's going on?"

"Going out. Ça sufit. I'd rather just die. The idea of an eternity, even an extra ten or twenty years thinking about, dreaming about the Ile San Luis, Gretta, when I was twenty, the Uffizi Gallery in Florence at twenty-one, Dolores Volini at Orchestra Hall in Chicago, box seats, Rachmaninoff's Variations on a Theme by Paganinni, my grandmother's potato pancakes around Christmas/Chanuka, my Brazilian wife's ankles the first night I saw her, Glenna and her patté and whole-wheat crackers, deer in the driveway, the first snow, Audrey Hepburn in Roman Holiday, Dietrich in Kismet, those golden legs..."

"I think you might need some counseling. Mabe I should call..."

"Call this!"

Threatening to hit him on his conker with his cane, "Wiedersehen, Adios, Adieu...why didn't my grandmother teach me more Czech..."

The doctor turns, let's him go, turns himself and goes back into his office and turns on his e-Mac. Internet search. Then turns it off, puts on his coat, there's this great German bar down the street. No Chinese additives, just genius killer Deutschland stuff. Hesitates. Waits until Mr. Battercane gets in the elevator and goes down, down, hopefully forever, down...

Credits

"Geneology," Salt River Review, 2008.

"Revoir," Timber Creek Review, Winter, 2008.

"Bethelehemania," Cantaraville, #3, April, 2008.

"The Book of Ancient Wisdom," The Big Stupid Review, Cold Drill Press, 10-01-2007.

"Monkeyshine," GUD magazine, Issue 2, Spring 2008.

"What Do You Do On Sundays?," Cadillac Cicatrix, Vol.1, #2, 2007. (A piece taken from volume What Do You Do On Sundays?)

"Miriam Meets Father Peguy," Timber Creek Review. Vol.13, #1, Spring 2007. (Originally a chapter from the novel The Depths and the Dragons

"Nothing Left to Fall," Delivered (England), June, 2008, Karamu, Spring, 2009.

"Links," Chiron Review.

"Shhhhhhhh," Askew Reviews, #13, Spring, 2008.

"Immortal Jaguar," Takahe 65 (New Zealand), 2008. Issue 3.

"A Little Pencil Magic," Sketchbook, #3, May 5, 2008.

"Essences," Grits, #2, February, 2009 (on line).

About the Author

Hugh Fox was born in Chicago in 1932. He spent his childhood studying violin, piano, composition and opera with his Viennese teacher Zerlina Muhlman Metzger. He received a M.A. degree in English from Loyola University in Chicago and his Ph.D. in American Literature from the University of Illinois (Urbana-Champaign).

He met his first wife, a Peruvian woman named Lucia Ungaro de Zevallos, while at Urbana-Campaign. Hugh was a Professor of American Literature from 1958-1968 at Loyola University in Los Angeles. He became a Professor in the Department of American Thought and Language at Michigan State University in 1968 and remained there until he retired in 1999.

It was at MSU that he met his second wife Nona Grimes. They were married in 1970. He received Fulbright Professsorships at the University of Hermosillo in Mexico in 1961, the Instituto Pedagogico and Universidad Catolica in Caracas from 1964 to 1966, and at the University of Santa Catarina in Brazil from 1978-1980. He met his third wife Maria Bernadete Costa in Brazil in 1978. They've been married for 28 years.

He studied Latin American literature at the University of Buenos Aires on and OAS grant and spent a year as an archaeologist in the Atacama Desert in Chile in 1986. He was the founder and Board of Directors member of COSMEP, the International Organization of Independent Publishers, from 1968 until its death in 1996.

Editor of *Ghost Dance: The International Quarterly of Experimental Poetry* from 1968-1995. Latin American editor of *Western World Review* & *North American Review*, during the 60's. Former contributing reviewer on *Smith/ Pulpsmith*, Choice etc. currently contributing reviewer to *SPR* and *SMR*. Listed in *Who's Who: The Two Thousand Most Important Writers in the Last Millenium*, *Dictionary of Middlewestern Writers*, and *The International Who's Who*. He has 85 books published and has another 30 (mainly the novels and plays and one archaeology book) still unpublished on the shelves.